CW00621682

JENIKA SNOW

Evernight Publishing

www.evernightpublishing.com

Copyright© 2016

Jenika Snow

Editor: Karyn White

Cover Artist: Sour Cherry Designs

Jacket Design: Jay Aheer

ISBN: 978-1-77233-725-9

ALL RIGHTS RESERVED

JENIKA SNOW

DEDICATION

For everyone who likes a bad boy.

I want to give a big thank you to the readers, because you guys rock! A thank you to my family for supporting me, for my mother who was the most incredible person on this planet. I also want to thank everyone at Evernight because they are insanely great in all ways.

JENIKA SNOW

DENYING THE BAD BOY

Tattooed and Pierced, 2

Jenika Snow

Copyright © 2013

Chapter One

The asshole clocked Alex in the jaw, and immediately a tangy, metallic flavor filled his mouth. He turned his head, spit out the blood, and turned back to Karson. Alex shouldn't have had so much to drink, and he certainly shouldn't have hit on the beefy wrestler's girlfriend, especially when he knew Karson had one hell of a temper, but damn she looked good and had been eye-fucking him the whole night. How could someone expect a guy not to notice a girl wearing clothes so tight he could see her fucking nipples through her shirt, or practically make out the outline of her pussy when she bent over? He was only human for fuck's sake.

"You're a stupid fucking prick, and I'm going to enjoy knocking your ass down." Alex hadn't been aiming to fuck her, but shit, a little flirting never hurt … not until right now. Karson rolled his head on his shoulders and cracked his knuckles. Alex may have a good three inches on the wrestler's six foot frame, but Karson was a thick asshole from four years of college wrestling. Hell, the guy didn't even have a neck.

The frat house party was in full swing still, but a horde of people had congregated around them. Their excitement to see more bloodshed was tangible, and the pounding bass of the rap music, and the spectators' hollers and yells for them to throw another punch, had adrenalin pounding through Alex's veins. The alcohol became a dim entity inside of him, and he straightened to his full six-foot-three height, rolled his shoulders, and got ready to get dirty. Yeah, he started this shit, but he was about to end it. He would not look like some kind of pussy, not when he could hold his own.

"Well, come on then." Karson's face turned a deep shade of red, not something that looked particularly good with his bright red hair. The burly fucker charged him and started swinging, his anger causing his movements to be sloppy and uncoordinated. Alex may have had a good buzz going on, but he had gotten into enough fights to do this shit in his sleep. A fist came at him, and he blocked it. Bringing his arm back and then forward, he slammed his knuckles into Karson's jaw. The asshole's lip split, and blood started a slow trail down his chin. The crowd went wild, and Alex would be lying if he said he wasn't getting off on it. Their chants for more became a rhythmic movement inside of him, and he went after the wrestler. A right hook to the chin, and then a punch to the gut had Karson doubling over and grunting in pain.

"You fucker." Alex grinned when the wrestler stood again and bared his red tinged teeth. "You walk around here like you fucking own the place."

He swung, and Alex moved out of the way a millisecond before his fist connected with the side of his head. They did this several more times until the crowd got restless and Alex had enough of this fucking dance. He moved to the right to block Karson's blow, and then followed up with two hits to his kidneys. Karson went down like a big fucking sack of potatoes, and Alex knew he'd be pissing blood for a week. He groaned and grunted, trying to rise but instead wrapped his arms around his waist and stayed in the fetal position. Karson's girl came running up to him, dropped to her knees, and started petting his bloody chin. Alex didn't stay around and watch, and instead spit out another mouthful of blood and spit and pushed his way through the crowd. Several of his fellow teammates slammed him on the back and started giving him a play-by-play of the fight, like he hadn't been in the thick of it. He just kept moving.

The frat house was filled to the brim with students from OSU as well as a few of the smaller colleges in Columbus. A girl wrapped her arms around his neck and pressed her tits into his side.

"Alex." Her whiny, slurred voice and the stench of the buttery nipples she had been downing told him she was drunker than shit, which was an immediate turnoff. Unhooking her arms from him, he gently pushed her away. She pouted her red painted lips and took a step closer to him. He shook his head. "But why? You've slept with half the girls here. Am I not hot enough?"

So what if he liked to fuck? It was a natural desire for humans, but the chicks he slept with had never been drunk. That was where he drew the line. For one thing it shriveled up his dick when they were sloppier than shit, and for another thing he had heard of several guys getting accused of rape during parties like this. He didn't want to be associated with any of that shit.

"I'm not into doing it with girls that can't stand up straight without weaving to the side." It took her a few seconds to understand what he was saying.

"I'm not drunk." She said this at the same time she weaved to the side.

"Kait." A little blonde came walking up to the drunk chick, whispered something in her ear, and

9

scowled over at him. He held up his hands, not about to be accused of taking advantage of anyone, and turned to head back into the kitchen.

The kitchen was packed, and a small line was formed for the keg. He didn't want any beer, but a shot sounded like it might hit the spot, especially since he had just finished that fight and his blood was still pumping. He probably could have found a sober chick to screw, but a shot of whiskey sounded more appealing at the moment. He really should just go pass out in one of the rooms since he had to be up early for football practice, but fuck it.

"Alex, my man." Kash Lennon slapped him on the back and held up the bottle of Crown. He lifted his eyebrows, and Alex grinned and tilted his head in a nod of acknowledgment. He had known Kash for the last four years, ever since he had started his freshman year at OSU. They'd hit it off right away when they shared an economics class together. Kash may be quiet and keep to himself, but people did tend to stay away from him, what with the fucker being nearly six and a half feet tall, covered in ink, and having his lower lip pierced. He looked like one badass motherfucker, but was loyal as hell, and Alex was honored to call him a friend.

"Fuck, dude, you look like you got your ass handed to you." Kash poured them each a shot. They tipped the glasses back in unison, and Alex hissed as the liquor stung his split lip. He gestured for Kash to pour another round.

"Yeah, well you should see the other guy."

Kash chuckled, and then they repeated tossing the shots down and pouring a third. Alex felt the alcohol start to burn its way through his veins, and the buzz that had faded during the fight started to take hold once more. The fight with Karson had dimmed the high he felt, and now he was anxious to get right back there, minus hitting on chicks with boyfriends.

"Don't you have practice at the ass crack of dawn tomorrow?" Kash leaned against the counter and crossed his big fucking arms over his chest. Alex swore the guy got bigger every time he saw him.

"Yeah, but it isn't like I haven't practiced hungover before." They both chuckled, but then their eyes were riveted to a hot blonde that walked past them. Alex zeroed in on her ass, and watched the almost hypnotic sway of her hips, and the jiggle of that juicy body part. He wasn't so much of an ass man, but fuck she had a big, round one that he itched to get his fingers around. The high heels she wore plumped out her ass even more. He was also a tit kind of guy, and that girl had that going on, too.

"Damn, dude, she is smokin'."

"You gonna hit that tonight?" Alex asked when he noticed Kash staring at the blonde who had now parked herself right beside the keg. Her pants were so damn tight there was no way she was wearing panties. Panties. Another fetish Alex had, and not one he was not ashamed of.

"Nah, dude. I fucked this chick last night and still am walking funny." Alex looked over at Kash and lifted a brow. "Dude, she rode me so fucking hard I thought my dick would snap in half." Alex busted out laughing. "You think I'm lying, but I'm not."

Oh Alex didn't doubt it, but it was still funny as hell.

"You always get the wild ones."

Kash shrugged, but the corner of his mouth kicked up. He looked back at the blonde, who was now bent over. Her ass was popped way out, and Alex pictured himself doing all kinds of things to her in that position.

"Nah, man, they seem to find me. Although I'm not complaining," said Kash.

"I wouldn't think so." Alex rolled his head on his shoulders back and forth. "Maybe I should just head home. If I show up late again Coach will have my ass."

Coach Marx was one hell of an instructor, but Alex knew his patience was wearing thin where he was concerned, and including a few of the other players, too. Alex was grateful for his spot on the team, but he did like to party, and when he did it he tended to do it pretty fucking hard.

"Yeah, I mean I'd hate to see you sitting on the bench during a game." Kash grinned over at him. "You need a ride or you walking?'

"I'll just walk." They clapped each other on the back, and he headed out and started walking toward the two-story house he shared with three other guys. He had met Jordyn, Racer, and Klein back when he was a freshman, and they all lived on the same floor in the dorms. It wasn't until the beginning of this year that they all decided to rent a house off campus. It was a hell of a lot cheaper than the dorms, especially with four guys rooming together, and he didn't have to follow the University's rules.

The whiskey started really kicking in he stumbled over his feet. He should have cut himself off, because he knew damn well it was going to be one hell of a morning. The small house he rented came into view, and he took the steps of the front porch two at a time, which was a bad idea since he tripped over the last one and nearly fell on his face. After righting himself he pushed the door open. It had to be going on midnight, yet the lower half of the house's lights were on, and when he rounded the entryway and walked into the living room he saw why. Racer sat on the couch, and a pretty little brunette was positioned on the floor on the other side of the coffee table. Books and papers were strewn across the table in front of them, and she was currently rubbing her eyes.

"Adam, you know this stuff. It's late, we are both exhausted, and I don't think any more information is going to stick in your brain." She looked up, and Alex was struck by the intensity of her blue eyes. Adam "Racer" McNamara was on his fifth year at OSU because he couldn't decide what he wanted to be when he grew up. He had a shit load of credits, but they were so random and spread out that Alex didn't even think he had one degree under his belt. Why anyone would want to hang around and dish out tuition was beyond him, but then again as he looked at the gorgeous brunette he could see the appeal.

"All right, it is late. You sure you're not too tired to drive? I can take you home if you want."

She stood, and so did Racer. It was funny as hell watching his roommate become all flustered over some chick, but Alex didn't deny she was hot as fuck. She wore a pair of cutoff shorts, and her long legs were the color of peaches and cream. Her t-shirt wasn't tight enough that he could see a whole lot, and although that was a little disappointing, he also liked the fact she wasn't like half the girls around campus that seemed to be in competition for "who can wear the tightest shirt".

She grabbed her bags and turned back to Racer. Alex should really leave, but for some reason he was standing here like some kind of weirdo, and checking out some girl that he didn't even know. He could blame it on being drunk, because he was certainly getting there, and she was starting to become slightly blurry, but in reality he just liked looking at her, and not in just a sexual way. Yeah, she had a killer body with some hot fucking curves, and he liked the fact she wasn't stick thin. She actually looked like a woman, and not some anorexic teenager, a look which seemed to be growing in popularity with a lot of the girls that hung around him. There was some pretty filthy things flowing through his mind concerning this brunette, but it wasn't just that. He watched the way she lifted her long hair off her shoulder, and was transfixed by the way her throat arched delicately. He also liked the sight of her collarbones, which he could just barely make out through the V-neck of her shirt.

Dude, get a fucking grip. You have to be pretty fucking drunk to be thinking up sappy shit like that.

"Maybe you can come over again tomorrow?" Alex would have laughed at the hopeful tone in Racer's voice, but he was too focused on the girl.

She adjusted her bag on her shoulder. "I actually have to tutor someone tomorrow, and after that I have plans, but I can give you a call once I get a look at my schedule and see when I have an opening. It'll probably be next week, though."

Ah, so that was how an asshole had a girl as hot as her over this late. She was tutoring his ass. She waved goodbye and started heading toward the front door, but her eyes were on the ground and not on where she was going. Alex could have easily moved out of the way, but then he wouldn't have had an excuse to introduce himself, or to feel her body mold to his. Yeah, he was a shady bastard like that. She ran right into him, and he didn't bother hiding his smirk. Grabbing hold of her upper arms, he steadied her and inhaled deeply.

Well fuck, she smelled like something sweet and citrusy. His damn cock hardened instantly, and he willed the asshole to go limp. What kind of introduction would it be if his erection was stabbing right between them? He'd look like some kind of prick, no pun intended.

"God, I am so sorry." She glanced up at him, and the fogginess of the alcohol in his system dimmed enough that she was crystal clear right in front of him. Her eyes were huge, but in a good fucking way. She had this almost innocent expression on her face, and that only made his pulse beat faster, right at the tip of his cock. Her eyes were also bluer than anything he had ever seen, and reminded him of the Caribbean. God, had he resorted to this shit where he was comparing her body parts to places in the world? He was acting like a damn fool.

"Totally my fault." His voice was deep and gravelly, and he cleared it. Fuck, he probably sounded like some kind pervert. She wiggled out of his grasp, and he cursed himself. There was also no doubt he smelled like a brewery and liquor store combined into one. She smiled and went to walk away, so he spoke quickly. "I'm Alex Sheppard."

He held his hand out, and she looked down at it. He felt like a damn high school teenager all tongue tied and shit. He was just going to drop his hand to his side because who in the hell shook hands at midnight, or if they weren't going to an interview? Before he could drop his hand because he was feeling pretty douchy right now she reached out and took his hand in hers.

"Mary Trellis." She inhaled deeply, and Alex couldn't help but glance down. The cut of her shirt and the fact he was about a foot taller than what he assumed her to be five-foot-three frame, gave him the vantage point of seeing the slight swells of her breasts. And holy hell were they some awesome fucking tits. Big and round, and he knew they were natural. He could tell by the natural slope of them. His dick jerked behind his fly. "Yeah, I think I've heard your name around campus a few times." She smiled brightly, all straight white teeth and a little dimple on her right cheek. She also had a blush starting along her slender throat and rising quickly to her cheeks. He found the sight hot as hell.

Damn, he could only imagine the raunchy shit she had heard about him. "Big time quarterback, right?" He breathed a sigh of relief that she was referring to football and not because she heard that he banged one of the cheerleaders in the North stairwell. And then as she waited for him to respond, he felt *his* damn cheeks heat. Holy hell, she had made him blush by just staring at him.

You're such a fucking pussy, dude. Alex let go of her hand and took a step back. He didn't like how she made him feel: off balanced, juvenile, and horny as hell. A moment of awkward silence passed before she lifted her hand in a wave.

"All right then. I'll see you around." She turned and waved at Racer, who was leaning against the banister, and by the smile on the fucker's face Racer had seen his reaction to Mary.

"Here, let me walk you to your car."

"It's really okay. I'm just parked right out front." He was already opening the front door and gesturing for her to go out first.

"There are a lot of drunk assholes out there tonight, well, most nights really."

She smiled up at him, shrugged her shoulders, and headed outside. Alex was pretty good at reading people, and he didn't miss the way her hands slightly shook as she dug in her purse for her keys. When she found them she unlocked her doors with a click of a button. A *beep* sounded, and lights flared to life. Alex trailed behind her, his eyes trained on her ass, one that was the perfect size for his hands. The cheeks of her bottom shook with every step she took, and there was no way he could stop the erection that grew harder with each passing second. He didn't even bother trying. She made her way to a sporty little BMW sitting at the curb. He whistled low.

"Nice ride." He wasn't just thinking about the car. He had an image of her riding him in reverse, his hands on her ass and the cheeks spread wide. Fuck, he was so turned on. After he said something about her ride he immediately noticed a scowl on her face, but she did mutter a thank you. Okay, well clearly her mode of transportation was a sore spot.

"Thanks for walking me to my car." She smiled again, a genuine one, and Alex realized he really liked it. It wasn't fake or forced. *She* wasn't fake. There were too many girls that hung around the parties he went to that were fake as shit and only trying to get in his pants because he was the quarterback. He snorted at his thoughts, because it sounded dumb as hell for a girl to get in a guy's pants. Wasn't it usually the other way around?

"No problem." Shoving his hands in the front pockets of his jeans, he asked himself what it was about this girl that got under his skin. Yeah, he had gotten turned on by other girls in the past, but this attraction he had to Mary was bordering on intense and fucking crazy. He liked the convenience of a one-night stand, and he sure as hell didn't think about the chicks after they fucked. But looking at Mary, he knew she wasn't like any of the girls he normally went after, which also meant she wasn't easy. It wasn't like she had some kind of damn tattoo on her forehead stating she was the "hard to get" kind of girl, but she did have this aura around her that screamed she was way too good for him.

Alex could admit that at this point in his life he enjoyed only a few things in life. When he wasn't spending time with his parents and little sister Kiera, he was playing football, partying, or fucking. Of course there were always those occasional fights that got thrown in there, but that mixed things up a bit, and got rid of a lot of his aggression and energy he had deep inside of him.

He stood there like a douche-bag as she climbed in her car and drove away. He could only imagine what she thought about him, because he was probably thinking the exact same thing: what a fucking weird idiot.

When he was back in the house with the door shut behind him he saw Racer still leaning against the banister.

"What?" Alex all but growled, annoyed with himself and now Racer and his smug-ass smirk.

Racer shook his head and pushed away from the stairs.

"Nothing. I just want to say that if you think you're going to get an easy piece of ass from Mary, you should just give up right now."

"Fuck you, Racer." Alex shook his head, knowing his roommate was right, but not wanting to hear it regardless.

"I ain't trying to be a cockblock, but Mary is a good girl, and she really doesn't need the likes of you or me."

Although he considered Racer a good friend, Alex didn't miss the subtle warning in his words. He cared about the girl, that was clear, and he also knew the reputation Alex had. He couldn't get pissed at him for being interested in her.

"I can admit when a girl is too good for me, and she is too good for me." With that said Alex walked past Racer and headed down the hall to his room where he proceeded to pass out.

Chapter Two

Alex was right. There were a lot of drunks out, but Mary didn't really expect anything less. This was OSU territory, and it was a Saturday and only midnight. She had to really stay alert or there would be no question that she'd end up hitting an intoxicated pedestrian. Who would have thought she would have literally bumped into Alex Sheppard? They ran in totally different circles, were polar opposites in every way, yet she had stood so close to him they breathed the same air, and she could feel his body heat seeping right into her.

Oh, she had known who he was as soon as she looked into his hazel eyes, saw that they were more green than brown, and forced herself to not act like a hormonal teenager. Okay, so she may only be twenty-one, but being that close to him, smelling that spicy, expensive cologne he wore, and thinking about all the times she saw him but he had clearly not seen her, made her realize she needed to control herself. He was gorgeous and had a hard, muscular body that made her feel wholly feminine, but he was so not her type. For one thing he slept with far too many girls, probably didn't know half their names, and she considered him a bad boy in the worst kind of way. Just thinking about the time she had seen him coming in from football practice in nothing but a pair of loose fitting shorts had her body heating all over again. He had been sweaty and slightly red from running or tackling perhaps, but his body was hard and defined, corded and tensed, and the tattoo that started on his left bicep and covered his entire back in swirling dark patterns had instantly made her wet.

Then some busty blonde had bounced up to him, her boobs barely restrained in her workout clothes, giggling and muttering things far too quiet for Mary to hear, and that had been the end of that. Alex had wrapped his arm around her waist, and the two of them had disappeared in the locker room. Of course he hadn't even noticed Mary standing there watching him like a freak, and that was okay because she didn't need a guy like Alex Sheppard in her life. He was too dangerous and experienced for her, and besides, there was no doubt he would break her heart, whether it was intentional or not. Mary could see herself falling for him easily.

Tutoring on the side had given Mary an opportunity to earn her own money and meet a plethora of interesting individuals. Despite her family being wealthy, Mary wanted to do things by herself, to support herself. She took out student loans to pay for her schooling, and bought her own food and other supplies she needed to survive. When she wasn't tutoring she worked a few hours on the weekends at a coffee shop right off campus property. She was exhausted the majority of the time, but it was a hell of a lot better than depending on her parents to fund her way.

Her family came from old money, or so her mother liked to call it, and because of that there had always been a stuffy, aristocratic vibe to them and the way they had lived. But then again Mary was adopted, had been with the Trellis family since she was two years old, but had never felt like she really fit in. Her parents, Stephen and Marsha Trellis, had showed her affection when the situation called for it, but Mary never felt the love a daughter felt when around her parents. Her mother and father had always treated her like she was part of their family, but there was no denying Mary was nothing like them. She had felt that way ever since she could remember. Then there was her older sister, Margo, who was the most self-centered person Mary had ever come across.

When they were younger Margo liked to snub Mary, making her feel more like a thorn in her side than her sister. Maybe it was also the fact Mary looked nothing like her family. Where she had dark hair and blue eyes, all of the Trellises had blond hair and green eyes. If looking in the mirror every day hadn't solidified the fact she was so out of place, hearing Margo's twelve year old voice tell her she was clearly not a "Golden Trellis" had made it abundantly clear that she would never fit in. Of course, her mother had told her every night that she loved her, and that she was part of their family whenever Mary brought it up. Maybe it was just the years of her questioning her self-worth, Margo's hurtful words, of the murmurs behind cupped hands whenever she went to a social function that had her feeling that way? The years had gone by though. Margo no longer said those things to her, but there would always be a part of Mary that never felt like she belonged.

She took a left, and then a right until the small single story house she shared with her roommate came into view. She pulled into the driveway right beside Darcy's faded blue Corolla. Turning off the car and sitting there for a moment. Mary let the sound of the engine cooling fill the interior. The BMW had been a high school graduation gift from her parents, and although she hadn't really wanted it, and knew them giving it to her had been more due to the fact they wanted to look good, Mary also knew she needed transportation. So, she had smiled and thanked them, but hated every minute driving around in the thing. It made her feel like a fake and fraud, and she wasn't quite sure why that was. So, Mary made sure to send them payments for the car and insurance, and ignored their complaints when they received her check. It made her feel better knowing she could stand on her own two feet, because there would be a time when her parents wouldn't be here, and if she was dependent on them where would she be then? Margo took everything their parents gave her, and Mary knew when the time came when her sister was alone, she would drown.

Mary grabbed her purse off the passenger seat, got out of the car, and headed toward the front door. There weren't any lights on, but then again it was midnight. She normally didn't tutor this late, but Adam was having a difficult time understanding the dynamics of economics. Mary had a feeling he hadn't been paying attention either, not when his eyes had been trained on her breasts instead of the textbook.

Oh well, if he didn't want to focus on what he was paying her for that wasn't her problem. She unlocked the door and pushed it open, and immediately was assaulted by the loud, sexually explicit sounds of Darcy having sex. Mary rolled her eyes and went into the kitchen for water. Leaning against the counter and bringing the glass to her lips, she turned her head to the side and listened with astonishment as the sound of a headboard banging against the wall resounded in the silence. After only a few seconds of that racket all was quiet again. Mary finished her water, and just as she was about to head to her room a very naked Darcy and her current guest for the evening, Dane she thought his name was, came walking into the kitchen. The lights were still off, but there was enough of a glow from Darcy's bedroom light that Mary saw *everything.*

Darcy stopped when she saw Mary standing there, which in turn had the guy slamming into her back.

"Shit, Mary." Darcy placed a hand over her heart. "You scared the hell out of me. What are you doing creeping around in the dark? Did you just get in?" The nude couple didn't seem to be the least bit self-conscious over their body parts just hanging out in the open since they moved further into the kitchen. Dane opened the fridge and bent at the waist. Talk about an unattractive picture, even if he did have a nice body. She quickly averted her eyes and looked back at Darcy. Her roommate had started walking over to the fridge, and Mary decided now was a good time to get the hell out of there.

"Just got home from tutoring, and I'm beat. I'll see you in the morning."

"Yeah, all right."

She quickly headed down the hall to her room, and when the door was firmly shut behind her she breathed out. God, she so needed her own place, but of course she couldn't afford that on her own, and even if Darcy had a lot of sex, she was good company. There were far too many times she had either walked in on a lot of flesh jiggling around as Darcy screwed her boyfriend of the week, or heard the sound of their almost animalistic sex, or seen enough wieners in her house to give her nightmares. She supposed it was just one of the hazards of having a roommate that liked to get it on … a lot.

Getting undressed and changing into a t-shirt, Mary climbed in bed and closed her eyes. She was tired, but of course the blissful peace of sleep didn't come right away. Instead the image of Alex Sheppard slammed into her brain. Even now she could swear she smelled Alex. It was a darkly intense aroma that had her heart racing and her toes curling. She was insane, certifiably so, because there was no way anything would ever come between them. Well, maybe a one-night stand, but that wasn't Mary's style, and anything long term certainly wasn't Alex's calling card.

Oh, who was she kidding to even play with an idea like that? Forcing everything that was Alex out of her head, she made herself relax and finally felt herself drift to sleep.

****

"Sheppard, I want to talk to you." Coach Marx called out from across the field. Alex tipped his chin in acknowledgment and walked over to the bench to grab one of the towels sitting in a stack on the metal seat. He took off his jersey and equipment and wiped the sweat from his face and chest. Then he tossed the small strip of cloth over his shoulder and headed to where Coach stood talking with a few of his teammates.

"Damn, Sheppard, even hung over like a motherfucker you played like a beast." Harley, one of the linebackers and a mean asshole on the field, slapped Alex on the back and made his way with the other players to the locker room.

"You wanted to talk to me?" He stopped in front of Coach Marx and breathed out roughly, trying to calm his respirations from the grueling exercises.

"You came to practice hung over again." It wasn't a question. Coach didn't want any of the players to drink, because he said it polluted their bodies and made them sluggish on the field the next day, but he couldn't stop them from having a good time, and they just had to deal with the shitty feeling the next day. Alex knew in order to succeed in this sport, this career, he needed to kept to a strict regime and diet, but the truth was that as much as Alex loved playing football it obviously wasn't in his heart if he couldn't just stop the fucking partying and focus.

"Yeah, sorry about that." Alex didn't offer any more of an explanation. He respected the hell out of Coach Marx, but even nauseous like a bitch after drinking all night he kicked ass on the field. "I mean, we still played good today." It hadn't just been Alex that was hung over. There had been a handful of other players that had dragged their sorry asses out of bed and busted their balls in practice.

Coach ran his hand over his buzzed dark hair. Alex knew something was wrong for him to look almost hesitant. "Listen, I've seen that you're slacking in your studies, and have fallen under the grade point average that is required for you to play with the team."

Shit.

Alex knew he was slacking in some of his classes, but the last time he checked he was passing them all, at least he thought he was. Clearly he had been wrong. Although this was his fourth and final year at OSU before he could graduate with a Bachelor's degree in Sports Therapy, he had only been thinking about exactly that: this was his final year. He hadn't even realized he had been fucking up so much that he was now at risk of getting kicked off of the team. "Shit."

"Listen, this is totally out of my hands. You know the rules the university requires for all players, and the fact you need to keep your grade point average at an optimal level in order to stay on the team." Coach started pacing in front of him. "Alex, I have to put you on probation until you bring your average up."

Anger built deep inside of Alex even though this was totally his doing.

"Are you fucking serious?" His voice was raised, but Coach didn't even blink at his outburst. "You want to put me on probation?" Alex was now the one pacing. Football had been his life for as long as he could remember, and in one fucking semester he had fucked it all up. Yeah, he had read the rules which he had to follow if he wanted to stay on the team, but fuck he hadn't actually thought this would happen. "How the fuck did this happen?" It was an empty question, more for himself than anything else, but he said it regardless.

"Alex, this isn't anyone's doing but yours. You know how strict the University is about this, and it pains me to have to suspend you seeing as you're one hell of a player, but my hands are tied on this. All I can say is get your average up at midterms, and then when that happens I'll throw you back in the games. Go talk to the academic advisor and see what you need to do, and maybe get someone to tutor your ass so you can get your grade point average up." Coach slapped him on the back and walked away, cutting off any further conversation, and not bothering to hide his disappointment. Fuck, he was disappointed in himself.

Well, motherfucking shit.
****

"What time are you coming in?" Mary held her cell phone between her shoulder and ear and adjusted her shoulder bag. She kept her exasperated sigh to herself at hearing Margo's clipped words. Her sister's normally snotty attitude was to the nth degree with her upcoming wedding.

"Margo, that's like a month away." Her sister didn't bother hiding her frustrated sigh.

"Listen, I am trying to plan when the bridesmaids are coming, and I need you tell me if you'll be here any earlier. It isn't like you have anything else to do that weekend, or any weekend for that matter." *Bitch.* "Mom's having dinner Friday night, so I know you'll be there, but are you coming up any earlier?"

Mary gritted her teeth, biting back a smart-assed retort. *Just one more month of Bridezilla and all of this will be done.*

"Why don't you just tell me when you want me there and I'll work my schedule around *you*." Mary made sure to add a bite to the last part, because frankly she was sick of this high and mighty act that Margo put on. It was like the world would stop rotating if things didn't go her way, and at twenty-three her older sister should have grown up a little bit.

"I need you at Mom's no later than nine in the morning on the sixteenth, all right?"

"Yeah." Margo rattled off a few more things, but by then Mary wasn't paying attention. "I'm at work, so I got to go." She hung up before Margo could add another ten things she wanted Mary to do before the wedding and picked up her pace. With her house just a few blocks from the coffee shop she worked at, Mary usually opted to just walk, but only if the weather permitted. As soon as she walked into Just One More Cup, the trendy yet retro styled coffee shop, the scent of coffee beans and freshly baked goods filled her nose. It was going on eight in the morning, and already the interior was packed with college students. The few tables that they had were already filled with people, their books splayed out in front of them, and what was most likely already their second cup of coffee in front of them.

Polly, a newer barista who had only started about two weeks ago, looked frazzled as she wrote down every customer's order. Mary smiled and headed toward the counter. Polly let out a relieved sigh and stepped aside so Mary could take her place.

"Thank God you're here. I am about to rip out my hair." Mary grabbed an apron and tied it around her waist. "Kristen called off sick, and I have been here for only half an hour and am already about to walk out."

"You should have called me. I would have come in sooner."

Polly twisted her apron in her hands.

27

"Anyway, I'm here now, so don't sweat it. Mark comes in at noon, and he is the fastest barista here." She gave Polly a reassuring smile and turned toward the girl waiting impatiently on the other side of the counter. "Sorry about that. What can I get you?"

"Caramel latte, extra foam, and I'd like cinnamon on the top." The girl rattled off her order, slapped a five dollar bill on the counter, and immediately went back to texting on her phone.

Polly wasn't very good at taking the orders, but she was pretty efficient at making the drinks. They did that for the next few hours, and when the morning rush died down a bit Mary was able to slip in the back for a short break. She sat her ass down on a box and breathed out. She was tired, her feet hurt already, and all she wanted to do was go home and sleep the rest of the day away. Of course that wouldn't be happening. She had to help a freshman understand calculus, and God did she hate math. It was a curse and a blessing that she excelled in subjects, though, because at least she could use it to support herself. Mary didn't even drink coffee, and in fact she loathed even the smell of it, but the tips were decent, and the extra money went a long way in helping her.

She finished off the rest of her shift, and headed to the backroom again to change into something that was not stained in cappuccinos and lattes. Lifting her hand in a wave to Mark and Polly, she headed back down High Street and to her house. She'd only have an hour to relax before she had to head out again, but it was an hour she was looking forward to. The only problem was the entire morning she had one image ingrained in her head, and that image was of a bad boy named Alex Sheppard. It was like running into him had made everything so much worse, and even if it had only been last night she was already getting sick of wanting him. She had to keep reminding herself that anything that had to do with him was only going to end up costing her a whole lot of grief in the long run, which when it all came down to it was a ludicrous thought since there wasn't even anything going on between them. Ugh, she should just check herself into an insane asylum, or maybe join the Alex Sheppard fan club, because this shit was getting ridiculous.

Chapter Three

"Damn, that fucking sucks, man." Alex sat across from Racer at their kitchen table. He glared at his roommate, but kept his mouth shut. Yeah, it did fucking suck, and he didn't need or want someone else pointing it out. "What are you going to do? You kick ass on the field, and putting you on probation is really going to put a hurt on the team."

Alex ran a hand over his hair and breathed out. "I don't know what the fuck to do. Coach said I have to get my average up if I want to play again, and when I talked to the academic advisor she said the same damn thing. I am royally fucking screwed, but it's my own doing."

Jordyn came into the kitchen and headed toward the fridge.

Without looking at them Jordyn said, "What the fuck are you pussies doing?"

"Alex has his panties in a twist because he's flunking a class, and it brought his GPA down." Jordyn looked over his shoulder.

"Yeah, and? Why in the hell do you care about that? I know for a fact you have enough credits to graduate."

"I'm on probation from the team." Alex leaned back in his seat and folded his hands behind his head. At Jordyn's blank face he said, "I know you could give two shits about football or anything sports related, but I actually enjoy it, and being put on probation sucks balls."

Jordyn closed the fridge and went to the cupboard to get a bag of chips. "So what class are you failing? Maybe I can help?"

Alex chuckled humorlessly, and Racer and Jordyn looked at him curiously. "Human Sexuality." For a moment neither of them said anything, but then they both busted out laughing.

"No shit?" Racer took a swig of his pop and grinned over at Alex. "You should be getting an A in that class. I mean, that's all about sex and shit, right?"

Alex ran a hand through his hair and knew the strands were all sorts of fucked up. "Okay, so yeah, I thought it was easy credits. I thought we would just talk about sex and all that, but clearly that was not what the class was about."

"Dude, you really thought Human Sexuality was about people actually having sex, like you'd get visual aids and shit? What in the hell have you been doing while sitting in class?" Jordyn asked almost incredulously, but there was a hint of humor in his voice. "I mean, yeah, it has to do with sex, but shit, dude, I wouldn't even take that class. Who in the hell wants to learn about sex in society and all that shit?"

He should have known he was going get reamed for this, but he had walked into it.

"So I take it you guys can't help me out?"

Racer snorted, and Jordyn made some kind of grunting noise.

"Sorry, I can't help you out." They sat there for several more minutes before Racer spoke.

"What about Mary?" At just the mention of the little brunette's name Alex's pulse raced.

"What about her?"

"Yeah, man, she would totally be able to help you out. She's a tutor and all, and smart as hell." Well, things were looking up if he could convince her to help him out. "But I don't know if she has any free time. She's been pretty busy, and I would know since I try and get her to help my dumb ass all the time."

Alex knew Racer wasn't dumb, but he wasn't very smooth when he wanted to get with a girl. "Let me get you her number."

"You're just giving the chick's number out without even asking her?" Jordyn might sleep around a lot, but he was a decent guy.

Racer gave him a "duh" look. "She posted her number in the student lounge. I mean how the hell do you think I got it?" Racer rattled off the digits, and Alex programmed them in his phone. He would definitely be calling her later. Not only would he get help to pass his class, he would also get a little eye-candy while doing it.
****

Mary counted the last bill and smiled. She had made a hundred bucks in just the past two days, and her little stockpile of "just in case money" was filling out nicely. She shoved the money in her purse and made a mental note to go to the bank after classes tomorrow. It was already after five, and with tomorrow being Monday and her first class being at eight in the morning, she planned on going to bed before the sun even set. She stood and walked over to her bed. It wasn't even made, and the sheets and comforter were in a tight ball in the center of the mattress. Not caring because she was just too damn exhausted, she did a belly flop right in her bed.

A contented sigh left her, and she closed her eyes. Maybe she should just take a little nap? That sounded like a plan to her, but of course her phone chose that moment to ring. She blindly reached over to her bedside table and felt the edge of her phone graze her fingertips. Cracking an eye open and staring at the screen, she saw the wide, smiling face of her mother.

"Hello?" Mary rolled onto her back and grimaced as the ball of material bunched right under her spine.

"Are you sleeping at five in the afternoon, Mary?" Her mom's voice was filled with authority, and Mary breathed out, not caring if it sounded exasperated.

"Yes, Mom. I have been working a lot these past few weeks and am tired."

"Hmm." Mary knew what was coming and didn't bother stopping her mom from going there. It was a repetitive conversation, and one that wouldn't be over with anytime soon. "Mary Sandra Trellis, if you just let your father and me pay for everything you wouldn't have to be living in that horrid little house, and scrounging to survive. I mean, it isn't healthy for you, and it also makes us look bad." Stephen and Marsha Trellis did not like anyone in their family looking less socially acceptable than they were. And to them the way Mary was living was akin to a homeless person under a bridge.

"Please, I don't want to hear whatever you're about to say." Her mom made a sound, and Mary knew if she hadn't said something Marsha would have gone on a rant about appearing regal and not like some kind of peasant. There had been too many times where Mary had gotten into a rather heated argument with her mom on the fact money wasn't everything, and standing on her own two feet and earning her way was completely normal and acceptable. Not to mention it made her feel human. She enjoyed working for the things she had, and everything she had she had paid for herself.

"Fine, I won't be getting into this with you over the phone. That's not why I called you anyway." Mary had no doubt today's phone call had to do with Margo's wedding, because although her mother called her several times during the week, it was either to talk about the wedding, about Mary's lack of money, or about something scandalous that happened at the country club. Her mother continued talking about the wedding, which

Mary was already so sick of hearing about. She then started talking about a brunch Margo's friends were throwing for her. This had to be the fourth pre-wedding gathering since her sister announced getting engaged last year. It was a pointless gathering, and just an excuse for them to throw another brunch. Chanel and Heather, Margo's maid of honor and bridesmaid, had been close friends with her sister for years, and were clearly held in higher regard since Mary was at the bottom of the bridesmaids list. It didn't matter in the long run, and Mary even wished she was just a nondescript guest.

"Mary, honey, are you even listening to me?"

"Yes, Mom." Mary grabbed a pillow and shoved it under her head, because she knew damn well this conversation was just getting started.

"You've talked to Margo about everything?"

"Yes, Mom."

"Okay, very good. Now, have you found a date for the wedding?" May closed her eyes, a little surprised it took her mother this long to bring up the issue with a date.

"I don't need to bring a date. Me showing up should be good enough. Besides, won't I be too busy doing wedding things to pay attention to someone else?" Normally the wedding party just stuck with each other: the bridesmaids with the groomsmen. But Marsha was intent on Mary bringing a date. Her mother sighed loudly, and Mary rolled her eyes. Marsha Trellis was dramatic about *everything*. She supposed that's where Margo got it from.

"Mary, do you want to be the only woman there without a date? It'll look pathetic."

"I don't need a date, Mother. I'll have Chad, or Thad, or whatever his name is." Mary rubbed her eyes, and pictured the groomsman she had been paired up with.

He was perfect in that parted blond hair and blue eyes look. Hell, Mary even thought he played lacrosse, or polo, or something along those lines.

Mary heard her father in the background, his deep voice piecing right through the receiver. Whoever he was talking to it was clear he wasn't pleased.

"Listen, we will talk about this later, but you need a date. Thad is not a date. Going alone to your sister's wedding is just not acceptable. I'm sure there is a nice and respectable boy at your school that would attend with you." Aha! His name was Thad. At least she had almost gotten it right.

In other words Mary better bring a rich and gorgeous boy, preferably one who drove a luxury car. Maybe Mary should just find a guy who had no money to take her? Or maybe she should find a guy that everyone that ran in her parents' circle would look down on? The image of Alex came to mind, but not because Mary thought he was less than she was or anyone else. Her parents would shit bricks if she brought him to Margo's wedding. He was a Hulk, with tattoos and an all-around bad boy persona. Yeah, he would so not fit in with her parents' friends, but taking him was out of the question. For one thing she didn't have the guts to even ask him to go with her, and for another thing even if she did work up the nerve he would no doubt turn her down. Surely he would have a party or something to go to during that weekend. He didn't know her, and probably just thought she was some goody-two-shoes, in other words the type of girl he tended to stay away from.

Her mom rattled off a few more wedding details before she finally got off the phone. Mary tossed the cell back on her bedside table and stared at her ceiling. It was an older house with fading siding and in need of a new roof. The inside wasn't much better, not with the stained ceilings, brown shag carpet that looked like it was from the seventies, and yellow tiled bathroom with a matching piss-colored tub. But it was all they could afford, and Mary called it home. Although her mind kept going on and on about the conversation she just had with her mother she found her eyes growing heavy, and before she knew it she couldn't keep her eyes open any longer.

The sound of something buzzing close to her ear had consciousness slowing claiming Mary. She opened her eyes and blinked a few times and turned her head to the side. A wince left her when her neck protested to the sudden movement, and she tried to rub the kink out. Her cell moved sluggishly across her bedside table, the blue screen lit up with an incoming call. The temptation to let it go to voicemail was right at the surface, because if it was her mother again, or God forbid, Margo, she didn't want to deal with the hassle. But in the end she reached for the phone because it could be one of the students she tutored.

"Hello?" Pushing herself up on the bed she glanced at her alarm clock and saw it was eight. Her quick nap had turned into three hours.

"Mary?" The baritone voice that came through the receiver instantly had her pulse increasing.

Pushing herself up, she was suddenly very nervous. "Yes?" She knew who was on the other end because she remembered that voice all too well. In fact, it had just been playing through her mind as she dreamed of a very buff football player.

"Um, hey. This is Alex." She didn't say anything right away, and he cleared his throat, as if he was nervous. "Alex Sheppard." Oh God, he thought she didn't know who he was. The hesitancy in his voice was almost funny if she hadn't been feeling it, too.

"I know who you are." She smiled even though he couldn't see her.

"I got your number from Racer."

"Racer?" She racked her brain who that was.

"I mean Adam. Sorry, it's a stupid nickname for him."

"Oh, okay." *Oh my God, he actually asked for my number?* A sort of girly giddiness came over her at that thought.

"Yeah, well he said you offer tutoring, and I was wondering if you maybe had any openings."

Her giddiness plummeted, and her shoulders sagged forward. Of course that was why he would call. Did she actually think he would reach out to her for something else? Yeah, she stupidly had.

"Oh, well yeah, I offer tutoring." Rubbing her eyes with her hand she was tempted to just lie back down, but the grime of the day felt thick on her skin and a shower sounded heavenly. "I'd have to look at my schedule and see what openings I have though. What is the subject you need help with?" Hell, she knew she would clear some time for him, because even if all he wanted her for was to help him pass a class, she would take it. Besides, he was *really* nice to look at. She had to be certifiably insane to want to spend time with him, even if it was academically oriented. Hadn't she decided he was not for her, and that he was bad news?

"That's cool." A long pause settled between them. "It's actually Human Sexuality."

Mary rolled her eyes. Of course that was the class. She had helped a few other guys with that subject in the past. For some reason they automatically thought it had to do with getting it on since the word sex was thrown in there. Yes, that had to do with it, but she had a feeling they thought they were getting easy credits for a class they would watch porn in.

Mary didn't bother commenting on that or her feelings on the whole typical male aspect of his decision to take that class. "Maybe we can meet up tomorrow and I can let you know what openings I have, and some other details on the tutoring? We could set up a schedule, too."

"That sounds good." A beat of silence passed, and she could hear some shuffling of papers through the receiver, and then the sound of something heavy falling.

"Fuck." His curse was soft but clipped. "Sorry. I didn't mean to say that out loud." Mary found herself smiling. "Maybe we can meet around lunchtime, like say noon or one? There is that sandwich place on the corner of High Street that we can meet at. It's called Rocko's."

"Yeah, I know where that is. I have a break between Calculus and Sociology between eleven and noon, if you want to meet then?"

"Yeah, okay." He cleared his throat again, and Mary found herself pulling at a stray thread at the hem of her shirt. "All right then. I guess I'll see ya then. And thanks again for taking the time and all that."

They disconnected, and she let herself fall back on the bed. The shadows from the setting sun washed across her cracked and stained ceiling in swoops and swirls of patterns. A thought occurred to her, and even though she should have pushed it aside, she played with it. Her going rate for tutoring was twenty dollars an hour, but maybe Alex would like to compromise on all of that, because what she wanted from him had nothing to do with monetary value.

Chapter Four

Alex sat at one of the patio tables outside of Rocko's. Although September was technically fall the weather was still in the high eighties, like it was today. His iced tea sat in front of him, and the condensation left a ring of moisture on the white paper tablecloth. His heart raced, and he felt like a fucking pussy for the excitement inside of him at seeing Mary. Dammit, she was going to tutor him, he hoped, but he'd be lying if he said he wasn't anticipating spending some time with her.

He couldn't quite place why he had this sudden, almost instant infatuation with her, but damn if he could just switch it off. Usually when he was drawn to a female it was only for a few hours, just enough time to get her off and shoot his load. But he never had this desire, no, this *need* to want to see a female. It made him feel irrational, like some kind of teenage girl who couldn't control her emotions. Besides, Mary Trellis wasn't the type of girl he went for, and he had a feeling she wasn't into guys like him: ones that partied, obviously failed classes, and fucked far too many girls to make him seem like a decent guy

Feeling resolution that he would put Mary and everything that had to do with wanting her out of his head he leaned back in the white plastic chair. The waitress made the second pass by his table and grinned down at him. Alex knew that look. It was one of interest, and what better way to put Mary and her hot little body of his head than by hooking up with a random chick? Shit, sometimes he even disgusted himself.

"Hey, aren't you Alex Sheppard?" He leaned forward and rested his forearms on the wrought iron table. She wore a tight as sin white t-shirt, and the white bra she wore underneath stood out in stark contrast. Her nipples were hard, too, and Alex didn't make it a secret as to what he was eyeing as he lowered his gaze to her chest.

"Yeah. What's your name?" Her cheeks turned a shade of pink, and he knew that she would be in the bag if he laid it on just a little thicker. She was shy, but not shy enough that she hadn't had the balls to talk to him.

She ducked her head and lifted her hand to tuck a strand of reddish hair behind her ear. "Jessica Locker." She looked young, but legal, which made her game. "I just started at OSU, but everyone talks about you." Her cheeks turned even redder, and he knew she was embarrassed by what she just said. "I mean, not that I sit there and talk about you, but well, you know, everyone knows you're a really good player, and well, they all talk."

She rambled on, and he couldn't help but grin. He loved the innocent ones, and maybe that made him the biggest asshole alive, but he'd treat her real good, and then she'd have a nice memory of getting fucked her freshman year. And that's what Alex did. He fucked, nothing more, nothing less. The girls that wanted more didn't come looking for him, and that was just how he liked it.

"So, Jessica, you been to a frat party?" She opened her mouth to answer, but the sound of someone clearing their throat right behind him had Alex looking over his shoulder. Mary stood there, the little sundress she wore billowing around her thighs when the wind picked up. Fucking hell she looked good. The smell of the soap she used filled his nose, and that was all it took for his dick to get hard.

Weren't you supposed to kick the idea of wanting her to the back of your damn mind? He couldn't see her blue eyes because the dark Jackie-O sunglasses shielded them completely, but he could practically hear the condescending thoughts coming from her. How much had she heard or seen? For some reason he didn't want her thinking of him as this massive partying, fighting man-whore, despite that being the God's honest truth of who and what he was.

"I'm not interrupting, am I?" Mary asked, but again he couldn't gauge her reaction with those big-ass sunglasses on her face, and her voice was neutral, bored even. For some reason that annoyed him. Did he want her to be jealous? God, he needed to grow the fuck up.

"No, I was just talking to Jessica." The waitress muttered something unintelligible before turning and leaving them alone. "Here, have a seat." He went to stand and help her with the heavy looking bag hanging from her shoulder, but she already had it on the ground and was pulling out her seat. Alex sat back down, and a strange sort of uncomfortable silence passed between them. "So, uh, about the tutoring," he said to break up the awkwardness. She took off her sunglasses, and her eyes seemed insanely vibrant in the afternoon light.

"Let me grab my schedule, and I'll let you know what days I have open." She bent to the side and started riffling in her bag. The front of her dress gaped open, and he could see the lacy edge of her bra and the sloped mound of her breasts slightly spilling forward. His dick grew even harder, and he shifted in his seat. He cleared his throat when she straightened, and she gave him a strange look. "You okay?"

"Yeah. I'm good. So those days?" He spoke too quickly, and his voice had cracked at the end, like he was going through puberty or some shit. Her eyebrows lifted at the urgency in his tone, but he needed a distraction. The longer she stayed quiet and just stared at him, the more his cock stiffened at the thought of her full, perfect handful breasts, and the way the wind blew the tendrils of her dark hair around her face. The long braid she wore hung over one shoulder, and God did it look good on her, cute even. She set her tablet on the table and started typing. "I'm not sure what your class schedule is, or how long you need to be tutored, so we should probably figure that out first."

Alex knew he might as well come clean about the whole probation thing, because he honestly didn't know what kind of time it was going to take to get him to pass his mid-term. He was flunking that class, and unless she was a miracle worker, or took the test for him, he was fucking screwed.

"Okay, here is the thing." He scrubbed a hand over his head, and then leaned forward, bringing his face an inch closer to hers. "I need to ace this class in order to come off of probation. My average fell below the restrictions for me to play." She stared at him for several seconds before speaking.

"I figured it must be pretty bad since you didn't say anything when I saw you at Adam's house." She smiled, and he felt himself return the gesture. "So, what days are you free, and we will start there."

He rattled off the days he had no class, and the hours he was free on the days he did. She wrote everything down, and when he was finished she lifted her eyes to meet his.

"Okay, so I guess you want to pass pretty badly?" He cocked a brow in response. "Okay, I get it." She looked down at her tablet and typed something into the calendar. "I can fit you in Friday, and we can set up a routine. Maybe three days a week, and at least an hour each session? They can be in the evening since that seems to be when we both have the extra time." She continued to stare at her tablet and bit her bottom lip. Alex was transfixed at the sight of her straight, white teeth pulling at the red, full flesh.

Well, fuck. He was either going to have to go find some chick to fuck, or jerk off big time after this. He was hard and aching, and the longer he sat here with her, the more he wanted her. His dick also didn't give a shit that he was trying to stay away from her. The damn thing wanted her like a fiend.

"Yeah, that sounds good. Whatever you think will help, and whatever extra time you have will be greatly appreciated." Alex was proud of himself for actually forming coherent words, Jessica the waitress came back around and asked Mary if she wanted anything, but after she said no Jessica wandered back inside, but not before she glanced at him and smirked in a pouty way. Alex kept his eyes on Mary, although he should have been checking out Jessica and figuring how he was going to get her in his bed tonight. "So, what's the damage?"

She put her tablet away and looked up at him with an adorably confused expression. "The damage?"

He smiled. "How much do you charge? What do I owe you, Mary?" She looked away sharply, and he didn't miss how her cheeks turned rose in color. He was curious as to why his question had suddenly made her feel so uncomfortable, or why she kept squirming in her seat and refusing to meet his eyes. "Everything okay?" He threw back the question she had asked him when she first arrived.

She cleared her throat and finally turned back to him. She still wore a pretty blush, and as much as he tried not to smile because he didn't want to embarrass her, he couldn't help it.

"Uh." Suddenly her napkin in front of her was very interesting since she kept unfolding and folding it. "I actually had something else in mind for payment." Her statement had his dick jerking violently behind his fly, and going from semi-hard to rock solid. All he could think about was her asking him for sex in payment for the tutoring, but of course that was a horny boy's wet dream right there. Shit, he could imagine her red pouty lips parting as she told him that his cock was worth more than any dollar he tossed her way. God dammit, he was such a fucking prick to be thinking about shit like this. She was good and clean, and he was a dirty bastard with a filthy mind.

He licked his lips, cleared the hoarseness from his throat, and tried to force his voice to sound halfway normal. "You have something else in mind?"

She nodded and started playing with the end of her braid. God, he would give her all the cock she could handle, and she didn't even have to tutor him. And it wasn't just about him being a whore, because he was fucking hard-up for her, and in a really bad way. It seemed like it took fucking forever for her to answer, but really it had been seconds.

"I have this little problem, and I think you might be the perfect guy to help me out with it." *Holy fuck.* The filthy things that came to mind had him feeling shitty, but of course that didn't stop him from thinking them. He didn't know if she was a virgin, but she certainly looked virginal. He also couldn't imagine her saying she only wanted one-night of bliss, but wanted him to be her first. Alex wasn't in the business of popping cherries, but shit he would have broken his rules for her. "So, I have this wedding next month, my sister's actually, and I am kind of being forced to bring a date." She looked up at him, but didn't give him a chance to respond. "It wouldn't be like a date-date, but more of you helping me out big time, and well, paying for the tutoring." Alex was stunned speechless.

"You want me to be your date to your sister's wedding?" That wasn't even in the same X-rated ballpark as he was thinking.

"Well, it's a little more than that. I…" She looked around before turning back toward him. Leaning in closer and lowering her voice she said, "I actually need a bad boy to bring home to my parents." His lips twitched, and he watched her irritation over the fact he thought this was humorous cover her face. "I need you to pretend to be in love with me in front of my parents and their rich, snobby friends. I want them to see your tattoos, want them to raise their eyebrows and feel scandalized. I don't want to be their cookie cutter daughter, and I want you to help me prove to them that I don't have to be with a Harvard graduate to be happy." She took a deep breath once she was finished, and he could tell she was expectant of his answer. "I'm just sick of feeling out of place with them, and since I am kind of obligated to go and all, and am being all but forced to bring a date, I thought you could help me out since I'm helping you out. It would only be for the first weekend in October—"

"All right." He hadn't meant to cut her off, but she really didn't need to sell him on spending the weekend with her. It wasn't about not having to give her money to tutor him, because that wouldn't have been an issue and he would have been more than happy to compensate her for her time. Alex anticipated the time he would get to spend with her now and then. Yeah, it was a good month away, but damn it would be a good fucking weekend. Staying away from her had just suddenly gone out the window, because there was a shit load of images that slammed into Alex's mind, ones that were not innocent, and that concerned him and her doing things that required a hell of a lot less clothing. Maybe wanting her in the dirty way he did made him a bastard, but he never said he was anything but. He would be good to her, make her smile and blush, but in the end he wanted more from her. One night might not be enough, but it would have to be, because that was all Alex could guarantee anyone.

"Really? I thought I'd have to lay it on thick, you know, really talk you into going." Her cheeks were red, and he grinned.

"Nah, I'm all about going. I get tutored by a gorgeous and smart woman, and I get to go to some swanky party. Pretending to be head over heels for you shouldn't be hard." He gave her a wink, and she glanced away quickly, her embarrassment tangible. "I'm in." She glanced up and smiled, and that cute little dimple popped up.

"Okay, well great." She started messing with her napkin again. "That settles that then. So back to the actual tutoring. I can meet you here on Friday for our first session if you want, or is there somewhere else you would feel more comfortable going to?"

His erection had gone to half-mast during their conversation, but now the damn thing was at full blown hardness and threatened to burst through the fucking zipper of his jeans. All it had taken was her asking him to go somewhere else, and he had only been able to think of that one thing.

"Could we possibly do this at my house?" A rush of testosterone moved through his veins when he saw the pink coloring that covered her chest and neck grow a deeper shade of red. Ah, so he wasn't the only one with his mind in the gutter.

"Wherever you feel most comfortable," she said but didn't meet his gaze. She went to stand, and he did as well.

"You have to leave already?" God, he sounded needy. "I mean, you just got here. Maybe you want to sit down and join me for lunch?"

She started playing with the end of her braid and stared at him.

"I actually have to get back, but thanks for the offer." Before he could feel like a dumbass she grinned at him. "Listen." She bent down and grabbed her bag, and slung it over her shoulder. "How about I give you a call before Friday just to make sure everything is still good to go?"

"Yeah, all right."

"I saved your number in my phone, and I know you have mine." She smiled again, and he couldn't help but notice the way her lip gloss glistened under the sun, and imagine what her lips would look like wrapped around his dick. She lifted her hand in a wave and turned to leave. And like a freaking creeper, Alex stood there and watched her go. Was it wrong of him to want to hope there was a big gust of wind that would blow her dress up?

"Shit." Scrubbing a hand over his mouth he sensed someone step up to him. Jessica stood there, her teeth tugging at her lip, and her eyes slightly lowered. Yeah, she was trying to appear sexy. He had seen that exact expression a thousand different times, and although he had found it attractive each and every time, it did nothing for him right now.

"So, uh, about our earlier conversation." He reached in his back pocket for his wallet and pulled out some money, handing it to her.

"Thanks, Jessica, but maybe some other time?" It was just a saying, because really he was only thinking about one girl, and until he had her no one else would sate this ridiculous appetite he suddenly had.

Chapter Five

Holy. Shit. Mary walked quickly to the OSU library on 18th Avenue, trying to get her mind off other things, but only being able to think about her little meet-up with Alex. It had taken a hell of a lot of strength on her part not to look over her shoulder. She had felt his eyes on her so palpably it was like he had been actually touching her. She was rather proud of herself for at least acting semi-normal, but toward the end it had been damn hard when she had *felt* the way he looked at her, like he wanted to do really wicked things to her body. It was also a little unnerving and distracting when she noticed his erection, which he either didn't care that she saw, or thought it was something that would go unnoticed. Even now, just thinking about the way his biceps had bulged underneath his t-shirt, and of the way his abdomen muscles had been clear as day through the thin material, had goose-bumps forming along her flesh. She must be a masochist, because the only thing Alex would be sure to give her was a broken heart. There had been plenty of girl talk around campus, and she would have had to be hard of hearing not to catch all the horrid details of the hearts he left in tatters. Mary found it all rather ridiculous that the girls around campus knew how Alex Sheppard was, yet they still ran up to him like he was some rock star. The red stone, arched entryway building came into view. When she reached the entrance she pulled the door open and walked inside.

Taking a seat at an available computer, she started searching titles for her courses, but concentrating on anything was pointless, especially when all she could think about was how her parents would react when she brought Alex to Margo's wedding. A lot of eyebrows would raise, a lot of gasps would sound, and slightly covered mouths would be obvious as they whispered how scandalous it was that she brought "trash" to their uppity little gathering. Maybe it was a bit childish to want to shock the lot of them, but all her life she had felt like an outsider, like the square peg trying to be shoved into the circle slot. A small part of her also grew warm at the idea that Alex agreed to go with her. For a wealthy community that her family ran in, they were worse than the ones they looked down on. They lifted their noses to the lower class, had the most scandalizing secrets, and stabbed each other in the back. But face-to-face they were all smiles and catty humor. Mary wanted to show them that it didn't matter how much money a person had, or what they looked like. They were still human beings and deserving of respect. Hearing her mother repeatedly ask about bringing a date, her sister's nagging about what she should and shouldn't do, and the overall anxiety that seemed to plague her on a daily basis made her feel unsteady and out of place Inviting Alex to join her had seemed like the perfect release.

Release.

Such a simple word, but it meant so many different things. The one meaning she was currently thinking about was the sweet release that she knew she would surely have by being with Alex. Mary wasn't a virgin, but she certainly wasn't an expert on sex. Alex on the other hand was, and that could be very intimidating. But no, Mary couldn't go there, wouldn't. She wasn't in the habit of letting her heart get broken, and she also wasn't the type to have random sex. Emotions were always involved, for her at least.

The vibrating in her bag drew her out of her thoughts. She reached for her phone, and the number that flashed across the screen had her stopping mid-stride. Why was he calling her? The only plausible explanation was that something was wrong. Anxiety immediately took root in her belly, and she slid her finger over the screen to answer the call.

"Hello?" She grabbed her stuff while balancing the phone between her shoulder and ear, and started walking out of the library in quick steps.

"Hey." Lance's voice was calm and unhurried, so all of her anxiety vanished. If something was wrong surely he wouldn't be so collected. But then that thought was followed by why her ex-boyfriend was calling her in the first place. She must have paused a little too long in responding, because he cleared his throat and started talking again. "I know, you're probably wondering why I'm calling you."

Yeah, she was. She found an empty bench outside and sat down, waiting for him to get to the reason he had called her.

"I was just seeing how you were doing."

Mary felt her eyebrows knit. There were a few students down the way laughing rather loudly, a dog barking somewhere in the distance, and the noise of someone's bass beating an angry tempo, but none of those things even held a candle to the loudness of her heart pounding in her ears.

"You called to see how I was doing?" Now it was his turn to be silent for a moment, but that might have been because her tone was a bit crass. Mary pressed forward, because this conversation had gone on a little too long. "Why exactly did you call me, Lance? I know it wasn't just to check up on me."

It had been over two summers ago since she had last spoken to Lance, and the memories were less than favorable. Anger, hurt, and betrayal mixed inside of her, and she was pissed at herself for still feeling this way. Those unwelcome emotions had been buried deep inside of her, and she thought she had moved past all that, but hearing his voice had brought up the memory of how he had pushed her away so easily, and made her feel like what they had shared was really nothing at all. He sighed dramatically, and she heard the sound of sheets rustling in the background. Had he called her right after he screwed someone, or maybe she was still lying beside him in his bed? It wouldn't have surprised her either way. She should hang up, yet she didn't.

"I did call to see how you are doing. It's been years, Mary. I still care about you." Mary didn't bother hiding her snort. She should have been way past this, had in fact, but then all it took was one little phone call to drag her bag to *that* place. "We are adults, have matured and all that."

Dead air filled the space between them, and she glanced at the ground. A pigeon landed a few feet from her, pecking at the cement and then fluffing out its wings.

"Are you there, Mary?" She gritted her teeth, not about to let him gloss things over. She might have been a pushover back then, let him get away with things that were inexcusable on every level, but not anymore. She didn't need to prove herself to him, his family, or even hers. Mary was now standing on her own, and living her life, and because of that had grown in more ways than one.

"Yeah, I'm here." She didn't bother hiding the iciness in her voice. "To be honest, Lance, I don't have much to say to you. I think your parting words back then were adequate."

He sighed again, which pissed her off even more. He had left her heartbroken and humiliated in front of all of the people she had thought were her friends, yet here he was trying to act like that had been so long ago, and it wasn't even a big deal.

"Listen, I already apologized for how I acted back then, and don't really know why you haven't moved past this. That was so long ago. There isn't any reason we can't be civilized to each other. Our parents are best friends."

Mary pinched the bridge of her nose. Why she was still on the phone with him was beyond her. She should have just hung up already. "Lance, I'm not getting into this with you, especially on the phone. You calling me out of the blue doesn't do anything but piss me the hell off." She felt her face heating at how angry she was getting.

"God, Mary, going to a public university has changed you. Here you are swearing like some kind of sailor." She rolled her eyes even though he couldn't see her. He had a lot of nerve thinking he could talk down to her. Had he thought she'd forgotten how he used to treat her? The time that had passed was nothing in the grand scheme of things. Right when she was about to tell him she was done talking he started to speak again. "Your mom told me you're coming down before the wedding. I was thinking we could get together, maybe before for lunch on Saturday? I know you have the rehearsal and all, but for old times' sake?"

She wasn't surprised he knew when they were having the rehearsal, not when he probably knew every aspect of what was going on in her family's life.

"No." The word came out so quickly and harsh that she was surprised with herself, but then again she was furious that she was still talking to Lance, and that she allowed herself to continue to do it after everything that happened between them. "Things are done between us. I don't need or want to be your friend, even if our parents are close. I've moved on, started my life, and am not thinking about the relationship we had. You decided on what you wanted to do back then, and so did I."

She could practically hear him gritting his teeth on the other end. Lance may appear calm and socially perfect when others were watching, but she knew the real him. Get a few drinks in him and it was like watching a grotesque science project. Her quickly morphed into Mr. Hyde. Of course that wasn't why their relationship had ended so badly, although she should have dumped his ass for that alone. She should have left him the first time he yelled at her while he was drunk, and said some very hurtful things, but back then he was all she knew, and she was such a naive teenager that his apologies had smoothed out things that should have not been fixable. Since starting at OSU she had come to realize a lot of things, mainly that she didn't need a man in her life to feel whole. She supposed that was the only thing she had to thank Lance for, because if they hadn't broken up the way they did things would have been very different in her life, that she was sure of.

"I'm not asking for anything more than you're willing to give. I just want to be your friend again, like we were before everything happened."

What pissed her off the most was the fact Lance had never once told her he made a mistake. It was bad enough she had caught him screwing her best friend, but even worse when she found out all of their "friends" had known about what was going on. So there she had stood, watching in disgust as the boy she thought she had loved had sex with someone she had thought was her closest friend. Hell, she thought a lot of people cared about her, but it was funny and depressing to realize she had been wrong in all of that. He had apologized, begged her, and promised her that he would never do it again. In the end she had walked away, and she would be eternally thankful she had been strong enough to do that back then. No longer would she be everyone's verbal punching bag. No longer would she allow a man to walk all over her, and smooth it out with a simple "I'm sorry". The only thing he had been sorry about was the fact he had gotten caught. That had been the last time she saw any of those so called "friends".

Mary may have gone back home since then, but she made sure to stay clear of the people she used to associate with. These years had taught her a lot, and that was she could only rely on herself, and that people wore many masks.

"Lance, I really do have to go. I'd say it was nice talking to you, but I'd be lying." He stuttered out something, but she hung up and threw her phone back in her bag. The only thing she could think about as to why he was calling her was because he was most likely not with Brittany any longer. Her whole body tightened as she thought about her once best friend. Last she heard, from Margo because her sister couldn't stop from gossiping when she came into town, was that Lance and Brittany were still going strong. They both deceived her and deserved each other.

Just stop thinking about it. You've gone this long without them intruding on your life, and don't let them start now. She stood, no longer in the mood to research at the library, and headed back to her place. Mary wasn't much of a drinker, but she could really use one right now. But maybe a good workout would do her some good instead?

Ten minutes later and she was closing the door to her room and sitting on the edge of the bed. Her phone started vibrating, but when she saw it was her mom she threw it back in her bag. There was no surprise that she was calling right after Lance had talked to her. In fact, she wouldn't put it by her ex to try to get her mom to talk her into seeing him. That had been a big problem with him when they were dating, well, one of the problems.

Looking back on her relationship with him she realized there had been a lot of things she had been ignorant of. Her phone rang again, but she didn't bother looking at it. When her mother was angry enough, or desperate, she was persistent.

After changing into a pair of stretch pants and her workout shirt, Mary grabbed her backpack and shoved a change of clothes in it. She headed out of her room and into the kitchen where she stopped when she saw Darcy sitting at the table looking pretty rough.

"Hey."

Darcy glanced up, her mascara creating dark rings around her eyes and her normally blonde spiral curls looking especially frizzy. It was late in the afternoon, and she knew her roommate should have been in class. "You okay?" Darcy leaned back and ran her finger under her right eye, effectively smearing the mascara even more. "Hey, what's wrong?" Her normally peppy and outgoing friend looked pathetically sad, and that was the first time Mary had ever seen her this way. Darcy sniffed, and a fresh batch of tears filled her eyes right before overflowing and making black tracks down her cheeks.

"I just got into a fight with Dane." By the tone of her voice Mary knew there was more, and could only guess what it was that would make her usually lively friend so upset. She looked up at Mary, and the tip of her nose became redder at the same time her nose scrunched up and she cried harder. "I heard from Meghan that he fucked some sorority chick last weekend." Well, Mary could relate to that, but didn't say anything until Darcy was finished. "I confronted the asshole, and he didn't even deny it. He even had the balls to blame the whole thing on me because he said I didn't get freaky enough for him." Darcy's voice was rising now, and Mary leaned back, giving her a wide berth. "I mean, fuck, how much freakier did he want me to get? I let him—" Mary held up her hand and shook her head, stopping Darcy from finishing that sentence.

"Uh, no, just no. I can imagine what the two of you did when I heard the headboard slamming against the wall."

This had Darcy smiling, but then immediately she started crying again. Crap, she should have just kept her mouth shut. Mary moved closer and wrapped her arms around Darcy's shoulders.

"I really liked him, Mary, like really liked him."

"I know." Mary didn't really know, but was trying to empathize with her friend. Honestly she had seen more guys come in and out of Darcy's life in the short time they lived together then she thought was even possible. She didn't judge, and knew her roommate was enjoying life, which was something Mary wasn't doing. Darcy angrily wiped at her cheeks.

"I know what you're thinking." Darcy pulled away from Mary and sniffed. "I have had a lot of boyfriends, but I thought he was *The One*. Turns out they are all the same, Mary. These guys only want one thing, and that's pussy." Mary was used to the crude way Darcy talked, but never had she heard so much pain and anguish in her voice.

"I'm so sorry. If it makes you feel any better I can relate to what you're going through."

"Really?" Darcy sniffed again, and Mary reached in her backpack for a tissue and handed it to her. "Thanks." Darcy blew her nose, and Mary couldn't help but smile at how manly it sounded.

"Yeah, I really do know how you feel." She didn't go into details with Darcy, but then again her friend didn't ask her to elaborate. "It sucks, but I can tell you that it gets better over time, and you'll find someone that treats you the way you deserve."

"Yeah, I know." She leaned back and looked at Mary. "To think I'm crying over some pompous prick." She shook her head and heaved a big sigh. "Maybe you'd want to go out with me this weekend, help me forget how shitty men are by getting drunk and dancing like no one is watching?"

"Uh." Mary wasn't really into that kind of scene, but by the way Darcy puffed out her lips, gave her a wide-eyed stare, and all but begged her without words to go with her, she knew she couldn't say no. Mary hadn't had anyone to talk to or help her forget about what Lance did all those years ago. If she could help Darcy forget about what an asshole Dane was, then she was all for it. "Okay."

Darcy's whole demeanor changed. She clapped her hands together and stood. "I'm excited now. Fuck that asshole, and fuck the guy who broke your heart." Darcy couldn't have said it any better.

Chapter Six

Alex slammed his fist into the red, scarred punching bag. His knuckles were sore from hitting the damn thing over and over again, but he welcomed the pain. Sweat had made his short hair drenched, and beads slid down his bare chest. He swung out with his right fist, and then did the same with his left. He felt the tightening of his muscles as he tensed and put all his power right into the bag. Keeping on the balls of his feet, he did a few moves, making sure his body stayed warmed up. The sounds of guys fighting surrounded him, and the smell of sweat and testosterone filled his nose. This was why Alex came to this hole-in-the-way gym, where the roughest of the rough trained, and where he could let out all of his aggression. The gyms around campus were usually filled with the same 'roided-out jocks who had big heads and small dicks. How many fights had he gotten into with one of those pricks because they had started shit with him for not wiping down the machine fast enough?

Frost was owned by Dylan Frost, a former UFC champion who had since retired at the age of thirty-five due to a leg injury. He had opened this gym to help other guys that had been like him and just needed a place to let off steam without the regulations and rules of the gyms around OSU. It was almost an underground kind of place, where a lot of big names came by when they didn't want the pressure of a chain gym.

"Sheppard?"

Alex stopped hitting the bag and turned to see Vincent, one of the fighters training for an upcoming Columbus MMA tournament walk up to him. His knuckles were already taped up, and a grin was in place.

"Hell, no, dude." Alex fully faced Vince and shook his head. He knew that look, and there was no fucking way he was going to get in the ring and spar with him.

"What?" Vince's lip and eyebrow ring glinted under the florescent lights.

"Don't act fucking cute. You know damn well why you came over here."

"All right, well quit being a pussy and fight with me." Vince was already moving toward the ring. Alex gritted his teeth. He was warmed up, but Vince was a machine, and knew a hell of a lot more moves than Alex did. The last time they fought Alex sported a nasty fucking black-eye and limped for a week No way in hell Alex was a pussy, and could easily handle his own, but shit, Vince was a beast in the cage, was training to be in the UFC, and could kill a man with a few strategically placed moves. "I swear, no kidney shots, and I'll stay away from your face, pretty boy. I wouldn't want you trying to hook up with some chick looking like the shit got beat out of you."

Vince was a cocky asshole, and rightly so since he was the King of the cage, but if he wanted to fight, then so fucking be it. Alex had enough adrenalin pumping through his veins that he felt the power flowing through him. Another fighter came up to him and started taping his hands. Vince bounced on the balls of his feet in the cage, staring at Alex with an amused look on his face. Once he was finished prepping he climbed into the ring and faced off with Vince.

"This time you're the one that's gonna have the black fucking eye."

Vince threw his head back and started laughing. "Well, bring it on, pretty boy."

Alex didn't wait, just moved closer, his fists raised and his sole focus on Vince. They rounded on each other, and in a quick move Vince and he were on the ground grappling. Vince tried to use a kneebar to get Alex in a submission hold, but he flipped around quickly and had Vince on his belly with his arm behind him in an armbar.

"You fucker," Vince said through a strained chuckle.

Alex could have broken his arm, or at the very least dislocated it, but that wasn't what this was about. Vince twisted and moved out from under Alex, and then he found the two of them in a clinch, a move that had both of them face-to-face, their arms interlocked together, and their rapid breathing identical. Alex started throwing close shot to Vince's ribs. Vince grunted out in pain, and satisfaction filled him.

"Damn, Alex, you been training." Vince grunted again, but in a seasoned move Vince was now behind him with his thick forearm around Alex's neck. It didn't matter how good Alex was at bare-knuckle fighting, Vince knew his moves, and was an expert at Sambo, a Russian martial art. Vince slammed his free fist into Alex's side, and he grunted. "I saw you at Rocko's." Vince tightened his hold on Alex's throat, cutting off more air. "Was gonna hit you up to hang out, but then I saw this smokin' hot brunette with killer legs." Alex felt his anger rise at the way Vince spoke about Mary. "You bangin' that shit, dude? 'Cause if you're not, I'll be all over that."

Alex saw red and was shocked by the force of which his rage grew. He was friends with Vince, but something inside of him snapped when Vince talked about Mary like that, like she was just another lay. Tensing, he used all of his strength to maneuver himself out of Vince's hold, spun around, and clocked him right in the fucking eye. Vince stumbled back, and a look of surprise crossed the fighter's face right before his own anger masked his features.

"Damn, guess I know what buttons to push." Vince rolled his neck on his shoulders and started bouncing on his feet. "So talking about that pussy is a no go, yeah?"

The asshole was baiting him, wanting an all-out brawl, and Alex was falling right for it. He couldn't help his reaction, though. He couldn't help the way his motherfucking blood boiled at the thought of Vince getting anywhere near Mary. In fact, it pissed him the fuck off to think of any asshole getting their hands on her. His emotions reared up like a fire-filled monster, wanting to take down anything and everything that came between him and her, but he knew how fucked-up that all sounded. Mary was never going to be his, in any sense of the word, but he grew violent at the thought of Vince or any douche trying to get to her.

"Shit, Alex, you look like a fucking beast right now. All you need is some smoke coming out of your ears." Vince held up his fists and beckoned him closer. Alex didn't want to do any fancy moves. All he wanted at that moment was to beat Vince's ass and get out all of this anger that suddenly filled him. He charged Vince and saw the fucker smiling. "That's it, buddy, don't hold back."

They came together in a tangle of fists and kicks, each one knocking the other in every available spot. Alex got hit in the gut more times than he cared to admit, but he got a good uppercut to Vince, causing the other guy's lip to split wide open.

"Motherfucker." Vince stumbled back and swiped his thumb across his mouth, bringing it down to look at the crimson smear on his hand. His face turned an angry shade of red, but Alex didn't give a fuck if he pissed the fighter off. Vince had wanted to fight, and when he started talking about Mary all hell had broken loose.

"What the fuck is going on?" The sound of Dylan's voice boomed throughout the gym, and Alex realized everything was eerily silent. Looking around he noticed all the fighters had stopped what they were doing and stared at them. "I asked what the fuck was going on." Dylan stood on the other side of the ring and glared at both of them. His short blond hair stood up on end, and by the sweat dripping from his body it was clear the big fucker had been training. "This is a fucking training center. If you assholes want to fight dirty do it someplace else, you feel me?"

Alex nodded and sent a glare at Vince who was already staring at him. "Go ice your fucking face, Alex. Vince, get the blood cleaned off the mat," Dylan barked out and turned, but not before he muttered something about young dumbasses.

Alex turned and climbed out of the cage and made his way to the back medical room. He grabbed a gel-pack from the freezer and slammed the door closed a little harder than necessary. God, he was acting ridiculous, getting pissed at his friends, and over what? Some girl he had just met? She was going to be his fucking tutor, yet here he was, with a fucking hard-on for her. He sat his ass on a chair and slapped the cold pack on his bruised cheek. Maybe that was all it was: getting between her legs.

"Shit." He ran his hand through his damp hair and hung his head between his shoulders. He was losing it, and going ape shit crazy on his friends over it. It had to be the fact Mary wasn't like any other female he had gone after before. She was just so good, clean, and wholesome. The chicks he went after were already there waiting for him, their panties down and their legs spread. They didn't wear clothes that covered more than they showed, and they certainly weren't smart enough to tutor idiots like him. The sound of the door opening had him dreading talking to Dylan about what his problem was, because honestly he had no fucking clue.

"Dylan, man, I'm sorry about that. I just snapped over some stupid shit." And it was stupid, given the fact there was nothing between him and Mary. He lifted his head when Dylan didn't respond and saw Vince leaning against the wall right across from him. Shit, he felt like a damn asshole, but he was still pissed that Vince had said that shit about Mary.

"What's up?" The nonchalant greeting had Alex straightening and eyeing Vince suspiciously. Vince grinned and pushed off the wall, moving toward him. "You were hella crazy back there." He opened the fridge and grabbed a gel pack from the compartment, pressing it again his already swelling eye. "Never seen you get that fierce." He leaned against the fridge and stared at Alex.

"What, man?"

"I mean, that girl yours or something? That why you went ballistic when I was talking about her?" Vince saying anything about Mary had him curling his hand into a fist and gritting his teeth. He looked at the ground and tried to calm the fuck down.

"Nah, she isn't mine. She is actually going to tutor me." He looked back at Vince who hadn't said anything and continued to stare.

"Yeah?"

Alex nodded, knowing what Vince was going to say next. The MMA fighter was a big motherfucker, and fell into the heavyweight category. His black hair was shaved close to his head, and his equally dark eyes never revealed anything. He was a scary bastard, and a fighter no one fucked with, but something had snapped inside of Alex when he was locked in the cage with him, and what started off as friendly sparring and grappling had ended up in him snapping and taking it too far. This was the guy he considered a close friend for years, but all it had taken was Vince saying something about a girl that he had only known for a few fucking days.

"I've never seen Dylan that pissed." Beads of sweat trailed down Alex's spine.

"Nah, he gets wigged out on occasion, but it's not anything getting in the cage and fighting out the fact he's pissed can't fix."

Yeah, he had seen Dylan fight a few times, and the man was insane in the cage and a force to be reckoned with, but his anger had always been controlled. He had let it slip when he saw them going at it in the ring.

"Listen, man, I'm sorry about snapping out there." Alex leaned back against the chair and rested the gel-pack on his thigh. His face throbbed something fierce, and he knew Vince had gotten a few good hits in on him, but looking at the other guy's face showed Alex had gotten his share of hits in, too. "Just don't say anything like that about Mary again, yeah?"

Vince didn't say anything for several seconds, but then he gave a tight nod. "Sure, man. I meant no offense, and didn't know you were that tight with her. Last I heard you were still dropping panties."

Alex winced, actually fucking winced at Vince's words, and what was the fucking deal with that? He had never really felt nasty for the life he lived, but right now he was feeling particularly dirty. He thought back to all the girls he had slept with, and the term man-whore had never felt more real than it did right now, or when he had been in Mary's presence.

"Shit, Alex, you look like you're about ready to puke. You sure you're okay?"

Dammit, was he okay? He was letting some girl affect him to the point he was throwing punches at his friends. "Fuck. Yes. No. Hell, I don't know." He felt like some kind of adolescent teenager that just realized jerking off felt good. He glanced over at Vince, and the asshole was grinning at him. "What?"

"So you aren't with that chick?" Alex gritted his teeth, about to go another round just for the hell of it. Vince raised his hands in surrender. "I'm not asking so I can have a go at her." He waited for him to continue but it appeared Vince was waiting on *his* response.

"Nah, like I said, she's just tutoring me." He tightened his hand around the pack, and the gel inside started to become warm in his hand. But what he didn't say was that he wanted her bad. Of course Alex didn't need to speak for Vince to read his damn expressions that were clearly on his face.

"But you got a hard-on for her." It wasn't phrased as a question. Vince tossed the gel-pack in the sink and stood to his full height. Nothing was said for several long minutes as Vince stretched his back and lifted his arms above his head. "Well, if you're not with her, then you can hit up Tainted with me tonight." Vince looked bored, but Alex knew the guy was raring to go. Alex should have said no to going to the new and hottest club in Columbus, but he needed to unwind, and get his mind off of doing filthy things with Mary. Yeah, he'd go with Vince, he'd find a girl to fuck, maybe take her in the back hallway. Or, if he was really feeling dirty he'd fuck her in one of the bathroom stalls.

But even thinking about putting his dick in another female had the damn thing shriveling up in his shorts. Shit, he just needed to be with Mary, but first he needed her to help him pass his course, because fucking her before would make a whole lot of shit uncomfortable.

"I'm fucked in the head."

Vince slapped him on the back. "Alex, we're all fucked in the head. But it isn't anything a little alcohol and wet pussy can't handle. So you in, brother?" Vince moved toward the door, but stopped right before he went back into the gym. He looked over his shoulder and cocked a dark eyebrow. They held each other's stare, and Alex knew he was waiting for his affirmation that they were hitting it up tonight.

Vince opened the door, and the sound of fighting and grunts filtered into the medical room. Vince waited for his answer, and Alex knew he wouldn't back out.

"Yeah, man, I'm in."

Chapter Seven

Mary pulled her BMW into the compact driveway of Alex's house. She cut the engine but sat there for several moments. Why was she suddenly so nervous?

Uh, possibly because you have been lusting after this guy every time you see him, and now you're going to be seeing a lot of him, close and personal. After she went to the gym and worked out so hard her legs had felt like pudding, and she had probably lost enough water weight to fill her kitchen sink, she had gone home and taken a shower with water so hot it could have melted her skin. A pair of jeans and a tee seemed like fine attire to go out in, but when Darcy had seen her clothes she made a scoffing noise and shook her head. She had all but dragged Mary back into her room and rummaged through her closet until she found a dress thrust in the back of her closet. It was a black, tight little thing, one that she had only worn once to a dinner with Lance. She should have burned the damn thing, but she had spent too much money on it, and well, it was a beautiful dress. Made from French silk with practically no back and formfitting enough that it actually looked like she had a figure, Mary had worked all summer just to buy it. Maybe not the best way to spend her money since she only wore it once and it was now associated with her ex, a guy she never wanted to think about again, but she told herself she'd wear it again. Yeah, that had never happened, until tonight she supposed. It seemed too fancy for going to a nightclub, but Darcy assured her one could never be overdressed, especially to this particular place, one that was known by everyone, but where only a select few could get in. But lucky for them Darcy knew the bouncer.

Yay for them. Insert sarcasm.

Mary was still a bit hesitant on going, but all it took for that uncertainty to vanish was looking at Darcy and the sad expression she carried when she thought no one was looking.

Darcy planned on meeting her at the club at eight, so that gave Mary a little over an hour to tutor Alex, and then swing back home to get ready before heading out. So now here she was, staring at Alex's house, feeling all kinds of anxiety and anticipation, which was dumb because she had done this type of thing a hundred different times. This was no different. *He* was no different, and she needed to remember that. She grabbed her bag that was filled with several books she had checked out from the library on Human Sexuality. Figuring they would start from the beginning since she had no idea what he even absorbed in the class, if anything at all, she made her way up to the front door. Bringing her knuckles down on the door three times she dropped her hand but instantly clasped them together in front of her.

Several long moments passed, and she lifted her hand to knock on the door again. She knew someone was home because the sound of loud laughter, and a football game on the television playing in the background came right through the door. She had sent Alex a text earlier today telling him she'd be here at six, so he should be expecting her. Seconds later the door flew open.

"What the fu—" Adam stopped midsentence and stared at her. He lifted his hand that wasn't holding the edge of the doorframe and ran it over the top of his head, further disheveling the strands. "Oh, sorry 'bout that, Mary." He looked over his shoulder toward the stairs and then turned back to her. "I thought you were someone else. Come on in." He moved out of the way, and she stepped inside. The house smelled funky, like sweat, old gym socks, and something stale.

"I'm here to tutor Alex." She turned around to face him. Adam shut the door and glanced at the stairs again.

"Oh, okay. He's upstairs primping."

Primping? "Excuse me?" Adam grinned and shook his head.

"He's getting all pretty for his date tonight." Something twisted in her stomach at Adam's words.

"Oh, well I wouldn't know anything about that. I'm just here to help him with his class."

Adam was staring at her strangely, and she hoped her sudden and irrational disappointment was written across her face. Before anything else was said the sound of heavy footsteps descending the stairs filled her ears. Adam grumbled something under his breath and headed back into the living room. Mary turned around and watched Alex making his way toward her. He wore a pair of loose fitting distressed jeans and a button down shirt. The sleeves were rolled up his forearms, showing off the muscular, tanned flesh, and the first two buttons at the collar of his shirt were undone. His hair was damp and the strands were spiky around his head, but that wasn't what caught her attention. A nasty bruise marred his cheek, and there looked to be a gash right above his right eye.

"You weren't waiting too long, were you?"

She shook her head, his words kind of going right through her as she stared at his wounds. "God, are you okay?" On instinct she reached out to him, but he took a step back. Mary was immediately embarrassed for doing something like that, so she took a step back herself.

"Yeah, I'm good." She wanted to ask what had happened, but it didn't take a rocket scientist to figure it out. Besides, Alex did have a reputation for getting into fights. Mary looked up at him again, and even though someone had gotten in a few hits, she had no doubts the other guy probably looked worse. He was close, far too close for her comfort because a rush of heat filled her. The scent of soap and a light undertone of cologne filled her nose, and she actually felt herself leaning toward him.

"Whoa, you okay?" It was only when he placed his big hand on her shoulder to steady her, or maybe it was to keep her away, that she realized what she was doing.

Oh my God. Heat rushed up her neck and covered her face. There was no doubt in her mind that she looked like a tomato, but whether Alex saw that or not was a mystery since his expression remained stoic. "Um." She cleared her throat and quickly looked toward the living room. Adam and a few other guys sat around the big screen TV watching a football game. "No, it's fine."

When she looked back at Alex he was watching her with a strange expression, and a tick under his cheek jumped. She looked to her right, into the kitchen, but it seemed there was some kind of card game going on with several more guys. Was this how it was all the time? She had only been here a few times in the late evening to help Adam, but it had never been like this. It seemed chaotic and crowded, and as if to prove her point the guys in the living room started roaring out at something that happened in the game, and the ones in the kitchen were swearing and talking about "eating out pussy" and "fucking chicks in the ass".

"Maybe tutoring on a Friday night wasn't the best plan." Mary wasn't a prude by any means, even with her upbringing. She meant it as a joke, but when she caught his eyes, saw something flash behind them, she suddenly felt far too dizzy. What was it about this guy that made her feel so on edge? Had it just been too long since she was with someone, touched by someone, or had sex? Lord, it *had* been far too long since she had any kind of sexual interaction with someone, not since the last time she slept with Lance. Just thinking about her ex put her in a sour mood, but then again it was welcome because anything was better than this arousal she had for a guy she could never give herself to.

"Sorry about them." He didn't look embarrassed, but then she supposed there probably wasn't much, if anything, that rattled Alex. "It's like this most days." He looked around and then suddenly seemed uncomfortable. *Huh, I guess the Great Alex Sheppard can be shaken.* "I hate to say this because it's going to sound like some kind of lame pickup line, but it is kind of crowded down here. Can we do this in my room?"

Her face instantly heated again at his words, because even if he didn't mean them in the way she was thinking, Mary couldn't help but imagine what they could be doing in his room instead of studying. Her silence must have made him think she was uncomfortable with the idea when in reality she was picturing all kinds of very dirty things. "There really isn't anywhere else in the house, and I didn't think these assholes would take up both rooms where we could have studied."

He glanced down, and she couldn't help but smile. She should have told him hell no to his suggestion, because heaven help her it had to be bad news to go into Alex Sheppard's room with him, where they would be so very alone. "We can go someplace else. Shit." He looked up and her and gave her a pained expression. "Sorry."

"Alex, really it's fine." Mary was quite proud of herself for keeping it together when she felt herself unraveling inside.

"You sure? I don't want to make you feel weird or anything." It wasn't like she had never tutored someone in their room before, although it wasn't really the norm, and the ones she had helped in their rooms had been female. The problem was she had never wanted any of the people she tutored. But then here was Alex, so freaking gorgeous that she couldn't stand it, and wrong for her on every level.

Just get through the next few weeks and it will be all good. You can go back to your life where Alex Sheppard doesn't even know you exist. The problem was she hated thinking that, hated knowing that it was true, and that his date tonight wasn't really a date, but his next piece of ass. That sour feeling that thinking about Lance had caused inside of her grew. She wouldn't be anyone's piece of ass, and if she let herself be with Alex that is exactly what she would be to him.

"Yeah, I'm sure." Her voice was harder, more to the point. Going out tonight was sounding better and better. Maybe if she actually let loose and had a few drinks she could relax and not think about unrealistic things? Things that would only mean trouble. "Lead the way."

He stared at her strangely again for the next several seconds, but then again her tone had been kind of sharp and to the point. He nodded once and headed up the stairs. She followed him down the short hallway and to the first door on the right. Her heart was beating a mile a minute when he pushed the door open and she followed him inside. How many other girls had he brought up here? She must be a masochist for thinking such things, because she suddenly felt so dirty, yet still aroused by it all. His room was small, but then again Alex was a huge guy, with broad shoulders and a frame that was so masculine it had her entire core melting. A large bed took up a lot of the room. A flat screen TV hung on the wall across from the bed, and a leather recliner across from that. Aside a few half-nude women draped over motorcycles, or in lingerie with football gear on, the room was bare. Yeah, it was everything she expected to find in his room.

"I don't really have any place for us to study aside from the floor, the chair, or the bed." She looked over at the huge mattress and forced herself not to blush. "The floor is uncomfortable as hell." Mary could only imagine how he would know why it was uncomfortable, and the nasty images of him and some naked girl rolling around on the ground appeared in her mind.

"The bed is fine." They stared at each other for a moment, and she realized time was being wasted over something so stupid. She made the first move, sat on the edge of his bed and got the books out of her bag. The sounds from downstairs were loud and obnoxious, but not nearly as thunderous as her beating heart. Alex sat beside her, and fortunately he was looking at the thick books she had set on the bed. He picked one up, leafed through it, and looked at her with knitted brows.

"Well, damn, these things are thick as fuck." The tension Mary had felt thus far vanished a little, and she couldn't help but laugh. "I didn't think sex was this in-depth." Still smiling, she took the book out of his hand and opened it to the first chapter.

"That's probably why you are failing Human Sexuality since it's not just about sex." Lifting only her eyes to his, she smiled at him, and a flurry of butterflies started moving in her belly and the lopsided grin he gave her.

"Well, I can't argue with you there."

For the next hour she explained how sex has played a role in society. She had to give Alex credit, he actually acted like he was interested in the subject, but she also reminded herself that they were still talking about sex, and therefore appealing to the guy in him.

"Well, our hour is up, and besides, I don't want to keep you from your date." She grabbed the books and shoved them in her bag.

"Huh?"

It was already seven, and she still had to get ready and head over to the club. Traffic would probably be a bitch since it was a Friday night, and downtown Columbus was also busy. She looked at Alex.

Mary didn't comment on the fact he seemed confused by what she said, so she just kept talking about tutoring. "You want to get together tomorrow, maybe at two, if you're free? I figure we can get two days in a row since I'm free."

"Yeah, I don't have anything planned, so it's all good." They stood there for a minute, and she realized it was a minute too long as the awkwardness settled back in.

"You did really well with the material tonight, Alex. I don't have any doubts that you'll catch on to this easy." His cheeks turned a light shade of pink, and her smile grew. Well look at that, she had embarrassed hulking Alex Sheppard. "Okay, well I'll talk to you later."

She turned to make a hasty retreat, knowing she needed some fresh air to help dispel the intoxicating scent of Alex that seemed to seep into every one of her pores. She reached for the handle of the door at the same time he did, and when their skin brushed together a shot of electricity shot up her arm. Their eyes held for a suspended moment, and now it was her turn to blush. Alex on the other hand seemed unaffected again, as if he caught himself actually acting human, which embarrassed her further. Before anything could be said, or she put her foot in her mouth and stumbled over her words, she hauled ass out of there and away from the one guy who was slowly making her come undone.

Chapter Eight

Alex followed Vince down the winding staircase that led to Tainted, the newest underground club in Columbus. It was more of an upscale, exclusive club, with a line that wrapped around the massive red brick building every day of the week. The club itself was underneath an old building, in the massive basement that had been converted for this specific purpose. The pounding beat of the music quickly approaching filled his ears and went through his body like a sledgehammer. The stairwell opened up to the basement, and they stepped onto the landing. The elevator that was located on the main level dinged, and a group of scantily clad females filed out. Their dresses barely covered their asses, and their tits were hanging out showing mile long cleavage. Their heels could have been construed as a deadly weapon. One of the blondes stopped and blatantly eye-fucked Vince.

"Shit, man. I'm takin' that one home tonight. Or maybe I'll just fuck her in the bathroom." Alex didn't blink twice at Vince's words. The chicks were hot, but they did nothing for him. The small landing opened up to the main part of the club. The lights were low, the air almost foggy, and the beats were bumping. Lasers flashed across the space, slicing through the gyrating bodies that were all but having sex on the dance floor. It was a new club, but Alex had been here a few other times with Vince. It was always crawling with chicks ready to get it on, and he was ashamed to think that that had always been a turn-on for him. Then he thought about Mary and how she had looked tonight. She hadn't been wearing anything revealing, just some jeans with holes in the knees, and a form fitting tee. She had looked gorgeous with her dark hair spread out across her shoulders, and her blue eyes piercing right into him. She had curves that went on for miles, and he loved that she was thicker than the girls he normally went after. Fuck, he had it bad for her, but it only made it that much worse when he had her in his room and on his fucking bed. Yeah, they had been talking about schoolwork, but he had been having a shit time concentrating since the scent of her was like a fucking drug. He had picked up bits and piece of what she was talking about, enough that when she had asked him something he could bullshit his way through it without revealing he hadn't been paying much attention at all. How in the fuck was he going to get through the next few weeks having her tutor him when all he could think about was stripping off her clothes and exploring every inch of her body? He ran his hand through his hair and tugged at the short strands at the base of his head.

"I need a fucking drink." He shouted to Vince, who gave him a chin lift in acknowledgment.

"Me, too."

They pushed their way through the throng of people and leaned against the bar once they reached it. It was packed as hell tonight, and the scent of sweat and sex lingered in the air. There were two bartenders stationed behind the neon lined bar. Their movements were quick and accurate. Vince leaned forward, caught the leather wearing female bartender's attention, and said something to her that made her stop and actually blush. Alex couldn't hear what Vince was saying over the loud beat of music, but he was sure it was something pretty fucking dirty, and something that would have the punk rocker looking girl dropping her panties and grabbing her ankles for him by the end of the night. Vince tapped on the bar twice, and Alex could practically hear the girl sigh. A moment later there were two cold bottles of beer before them, and the bartender was sliding a piece of paper into Vince's palm.

They turned back around toward the club. Alex leaned to the side but kept his eyes on a couple of girls dry humping each other a few feet away.

"Do I even want to know what you said to that chick?" He heard Vince chuckle but didn't turn to look at him.

"Not unless you want to watch what I told her I'd do with my tongue when she got off work?" Alex lifted his hand that held the bottle of beer and curled his lip in disgust. Vince chuckled harder. "I didn't think so." They stood there for another few minutes before Vince slammed his bottle on the counter. "I'm going to find myself a piece of ass."

"What about hitting it up with the punk chick?" Alex looked at Vince who was scanning the crowd. "I'll be calling her later." He looked at Alex and gave him a cocky smirk. The bastard always gave him a hard time for sleeping around, but Vince was just as guilty as the rest of them. Vince sauntered into the crowd, and the bodies parted before him like he was oil and they were water. Alex brought his beer to his mouth and took a long pull from it. He let his gaze sweep over the bodies, and when he made a second sweep his eyes landed on a redhead who stood a few feet in front of him. She was alone, her body facing his, her eyes locked on him. The shorts she wore couldn't be called anything but the booty variety, and her top was nothing more than a strip of elastic that barely covered her huge, most likely fake, tits. She moved to the music, and each swivel of her hips was meant to entice. She ran her hands up and down her body, caressing her breasts, and then slowly moving them down her belly, over her pussy, and started the whole process again. Normally he would have been all over that, but here he was, still picturing Mary sitting on his bed, and not able to get the scent of her out of his head. This was bullshit, and he was acting like an idiot.

He finished off his beer and set the bottle on the bar before moving toward the busty redhead. She continued to move her hips back and forth as she approached. He stopped in front of her, and she immediately hooked her finger around the collar of his shirt and pulled him closer. Their bodies connected, and he felt the firm, perfect globes of her tits against his chest, and the softness of her thighs met his. He wrapped his hand around her too thin waist, felt the edge of her ribs poking out, but didn't focus on that. Her perfume was strong and slightly nauseating, but she was a female, relatively attractive, and wanted him. He wasn't picky, especially not when he was trying to get a piece of ass and forget about a certain sexy and intelligent brunette who was tutoring him.

"Don't I know you?" She all but purred, and lifted her heavily made up eyes to his. She batted her eyelashes at him, and he was sure to other guys that look made them putty in her hands. To him it just made him even more indifferent.

"No."

She scanned his face, and he saw her red painted lips purse. Apparently she wasn't used to hearing that word.

"Yeah, aren't you a football player for OSU? I think I've seen your face in the paper."

It was possible, but he didn't come here to talk about his stats, and he knew neither had she, not dressed like that. He didn't bother responding, but did lift his head and scan the crowd again. Maybe he wouldn't fuck her? Maybe he should just go home and jerk off thinking of Mary? That sounded a hell of a lot more pleasurable than what he was doing right now. He was about to walk away and do just that when a flash of inky blackness caught his attention. The bodies swarmed in momentarily, and the flash was gone. How he even saw something like that with all of the shadows shrouding the club was beyond him, but it had been something that had instantly jumped out at him.

"Hey, you interested in me or something else?" They continued to dance, but his mind was no longer in this, and it seemed neither was his body since her sexual moves against him didn't even have his dick twitching. The song switched to something more sensual, slower, and with more bass. The crowd parted again, and that was when he saw a strip of peach colored flesh amidst the form fitting dark dress. The flashes of lights washed across her, highlighted the heavy tumble of dark hair atop her head, and her killer ass body. But when she turned to the side slightly and he saw her profile, everything inside of him stilled. His dick got hard instantly when he saw that Mary stood just a few feet away from him, her dancing drawing the attention of more than one asshole in the club, his included. What was she doing here anyway, and dressed like she wanted to be fucked? Shit, the whole, smooth expanse of her back was exposed, and the twin feminine indents at the base of her spine beckoned him. The material molded to her ass, and he doubted she wore panties. Alex lifted his eyes again to her lower back, and loved that she actually had hips, ones that he could hold onto as he pounded the shit out of her. He had always been a sucker for a female's back, especially those little dimples. The redhead pressed against him and moaned, thinking his hard-on was for her.

"You're a big boy, aren't you?" She ran her hands up and down his arms, and his skin tightened in distaste. She started moving her hand down his stomach to his full blown erection, but before she could palm him he gently gripped her wrist, stopping her. His eyes never left the almost hypnotic sway of Mary's hips. Stepping away from the redhead, he started moving through the dancing clubbers toward Mary. He didn't give a shit when the redhead started calling out that he was an asshole, and he certainly didn't give a fuck if anyone heard. All his focus was on Mary. There was another girl dancing with her, this one with a mop of wild blonde curls, but neither she nor any other chick in the club held his fascination like Mary Trellis.

Mary's friend's eyes were closed, her head was thrown back, and her arms moved to the beat of the music that surrounded them. Her friend seemed to want to catch the attention of others by the blatantly sexual way she danced. Mary, on the other hand, flowed with the music, didn't try to catch anyone's attention, and was oblivious to the guys that were staring at her like they wanted between her thighs in the worst kind of way. Shit, he was one of those guys, but the difference between them and him was that he was going to make it happen. Mary *would* be under him, and he would have his dick inside of her. Rage boiled inside of him at the thought of any of these pricks going after her, because she was too good for them.

Fuck, she was too good for *him*, but that wasn't stopping him from moving closer, or from reaching out to her and barely letting his finger run down the length of her spine. She spun around, her eyes wide and her pink, bow-like lips parted in surprise. If he didn't want her so fucking badly he might have found her shock amusing. She was in a club after all, one that wasn't ignorant of people screwing in the darkened corner, or giving blow jobs under the tables.

Alex gave her a minute to turn away and leave, because that would have been the smart thing to do, but after a second of her just staring at him he took a step closer until their chests almost brushed. Her pupils dilated instantly, and his damn dick grew even harder, which was saying a hell of a lot since the damn thing felt like it couldn't get any stiffer. He was a dirty fuck, one that had no business lifting his hand and gently taking hold of her arm, but he did it anyway. He yanked her forward, and she fell against him. Even with the noise all around them he heard her gasp of surprise. The heat that came from her, and the way her eyelids fluttered told him she was into this just as fucking bad as he was. Leaning closer so their mouths were only separated by an inch, Alex stared into her eyes.

"What are you doing here, Mary?"

He didn't phrase it as an accusation, but Tainted wasn't a place he ever expected to see her. It might be a place he had come before looking for a piece of ass, but it also was full of a lot of bullshit and a lot of filth in the form of dirty hookups.

"What in the hell do you think you're doing?" She tried to sound angry, but she had no heat in her voice, and also wasn't pushing him away.

He wrapped his hand around her waist and started moving with her to the now slower, more erotic beat of music. "Dancing. It's what people do at these places."

For just a moment she acted like she wanted to slap him, and that had him smirking. She was feisty, and that turned him on. The flashes of light that had previously swept across the dance floor were now absent as the DJ took everything down a notch. Couples moved closer together, started fucking each other with their mouths and tongues, and ground their pelvises together. Although he thought she shouldn't be at a place like this, he couldn't deny that the atmosphere, the look and smell of her, and the way she had now melted against him made him damn happy he found her here. His dick was a steel rod between them, pressed tightly against her belly and all but throbbing in time with his pulse. "So, you never answered me. What are you doing here?"

"Not that it's any of your business, but I came with my roommate." Alex lifted his eyes over Mary's head and saw the blonde now moving slowly with some guy with his lip pierced, a guy he had seen training at Frost before. He turned his attention back to Mary, saw her staring at his mouth, and nearly groaned aloud. "I thought you were going on a date?" Her words were soft, breathy, but he heard them nonetheless. Taking his other hand and sliding it over the small of her back, his breath quickened as he touched her bare skin.

"Date?"

She slowly lifted her wide blue eyes to his, her pupils nearly swallowing the almost iridescent color like ink spilling over.

She blinked a few times, and he watched as her throat worked as she swallowed. "Adam said you had a date."

Damn Racer and his fucking mouth. There hadn't been a date, not the way she was thinking. He had gone out for a fuck, that was all. There was no dinner, no hand holding, and certainly no kisses on the cheek when he dropped the girl off at home. He had a few condoms in his wallet, and that was about as romantic as he got.

Staring into Mary's eyes, wanting so much to be the good guy and not just Alex Sheppard, the quarterback that got laid a lot and didn't give a shit about much else, was something he suddenly wanted for himself. He let his gaze travel down her face, over the smooth, gentle arch of her neck, and further still. The back of her dress may have been nonexistent, but the front covered her up from mid-thigh to collarbones. But even that didn't hide her curves, or the soft large mounds of her breasts, ones that he wanted in his hands and mouth. His cock jerked between them, and a small noise escaped her. Alex leaned in just a little bit more until their lips barely brushed. He should stop, but was he going to? Fuck. No.

"This is a very bad idea." She placed her hands on his chest and pushed, but it held no real strength. "I'm not doing this with you, whatever *this* is." The smell of something alcoholic and fruity brushed along his lips, and that snapped him out of his trance. Her words should have been the thing that made him realize this was a bad idea, but it wasn't. Leaning back just an inch he looked into her face. Her eyes were half closed, and her cheeks were flushed.

"You drunk, Mary?" She shook her head once, and then licked her lips.

She blinked s few times and tried to take a step back, but he kept his hand on her lower back. "Why do you care?"

"Mary, quit answering my questions with questions," he said on a growl.

"I had two drinks." Her breasts rose and fell, making the already tight material snugger. He wanted her, and he needed to make sure she was right there with him, and not only acting this way because of the alcohol. He took another step back, and they stared at each other. It was a bit surreal given the fact everything around them was still moving, yet it was like they were in their own world.

They didn't know each other for that long, and him coming up to her like this, touching her and pressing his hard cock into her belly was inappropriate on every level.

When have you ever cared about what was appropriate? She may wear a frown, look confused as to why she was even allowing him to luxury of feeling her in such an intimate way, but she couldn't hide her body's reaction to him. Her nipples were rock hard, and that was clearly evident because she wore no bra. Her chest rose and fell forcefully, as if she couldn't quite catch her breath. And he knew, without a fucking doubt, that if he slid his fingers along her inner thigh and right up to her cunt, she'd be wet as hell for him. But she didn't make any other move to let him know she wanted to go the next step, and the fact he could smell the alcohol on her, even if she wasn't stumbling around drunk, had red flags going up inside of him like one huge stop sign.

"You've had too much to drink."

She blinked, shook her head and looked at the ground. For what seemed like forever all she did was stare at her feet, as if she was thinking about something really hard, and this one moment would define it all. When she lifted her head and glanced at her friend, he realized he was actually feeling nervous about what she was clearly going to say. Mary turned back around, and when their eyes locked she smiled slowly. It wasn't the smiles he had seen countless times when a female thought they could seduce him, but one of relaxation and heady lust. Fuck, he wanted her so damn bad, but at least he was with it enough to think logically and realize doing this here and now was a major fuck-up. Because as much as he wanted her, wanted to be inside of her and touch every inch of her, even this was moving a bit too fast for him … right? Shit, he didn't know. He was so damn conflicted. He should have never walked up to her and started all of this, and if Mary was as smart as he knew she was, she'd go running in the other fucking direction.

Chapter Nine

What in the hell was she doing? Mary stared at Alex, and realized that everything inside of her had stilled as soon as he touched her. She tried pushing him away, although it had been in vain. She wanted him, and by the erection that had just been digging into her belly seconds before, he wanted her, too. She tried denying him, but really it had all been for nothing. She was just as weak as every other girl that fell at his feet, but why did she have to say no to him?

Because you're smarter than half the female population that have been with Alex. He'd hurt you, and that would be a fact because your heart would become involved.

He turned and started walking away, and why, because she said she had two drinks? It had been after she uttered that sentence that he had closed off from her. But Mary should be thankful, because her resolve had slowly been leaving her the longer Alex had his hands on her body. The haze of desire slowly dissipated, and Mary was left standing there slightly cold and very embarrassed.

No, she wasn't drunk, but at that moment she wished she was. The two cocktails Darcy had thrust her way when they first arrived had done loads to help her relax. The atmosphere of Tainted was unlike anything she had ever experience. Mary had been to a few local clubs and bars since moving to Columbus, but this was like a whole other world. The darkness that added to the already sexually charged atmosphere, and the way people didn't care if others saw them practically having sex right on the dance floor was heady and already added to the slight buzz from the alcohol going through her system.

She was with it enough to know it was Alex that had touched her, that had nearly kissed her, and that knowledge had her wetter than she had ever been. Of course it was the alcohol that had dimmed her inhibitions and let her break down her walls to allow him to do those things. In the back of her mind she knew it was a bad idea, but her body was screaming at her mind to shut the hell up. He had let go of her, and she ached to have his hands on her again, to have his fingers brushing along the small of her back. It might not have seemed overly intimate, but it had been like flames moving along her body.

This was a bad idea, a very, very bad idea, but it sounded so good. The drug-like sensation that Alex had caused inside of her when he touched her body came back full force at that thought, and she found herself moving toward him as he leaned against the bar, almost seeming angry. He had to know that she wanted him. It wasn't like she was hiding the fact anymore, although she should. As if he was some kind of animal and sensed her presence he lifted his head and stared right at her. His expression was unreadable, but even more so since shadows from the darkened club slashed across his face. His cheekbones seemed more pronounced, and his chin squarer. She took another step, and another, until they stood toe-to-toe, breathed in the same air, and she was swaying toward him. Hell, this was so not her.

"What are you doing, Mary?" His deep voice was low and wrapped around her like liquid silk. He knew damn well what she was doing. He had been with enough women to know when one was coming on to him. That thought came at her full force, but she pushed it away. She wouldn't think about it, wouldn't let it take her under. She wanted this, and by the look of the bulge still pressing against the front of his jeans, Alex wanted this, too. For whatever reason he was holding himself back from her, and she would be lying if she wasn't a bit hurt by that.

"You're being coy, Alex." Lifting her hand and placing it on his hard stomach, right above the button of his jeans, had Mary feeling awash with potent arousal. She could feel the hard ridges of his abdominal muscles right under her finger, and when she started to slowly moved her palm up the muscles bunched in response. She looked into his turbulent hazel eyes and knew that she could easily fall for this guy, just jump off a damn cliff and never look back, and how crazy was that?

Turn around, Mary. Just turn around before this guy you hardly know ruins all other guys for you.

"You are experienced with women wanting you, right? I mean you do know when one is coming on to you?"

She didn't phrase it as a question, and it wasn't said as a slap to the face, but when she saw the dark look that washed over her face she knew she should have kept that last part to herself. His jaw tightened, and a muscle under his cheek ticked violently.

"Yeah, Mary?" His voice was low and deep, and slightly scary.

She took a step back, but he followed her move. Suddenly her pleasurable buzz was gone, and in its place was her familiar friend of uncertainty. A look over her shoulder showed Darcy grinding with some huge tattooed guy with far too many piercings.

"Look at me."

Alex's voice was right beside her, commanding and with an edge to it. She snapped her attention back to him, found him right in her face now, and parted her lips in surprise. He was so big, so muscular, and could crush anyone that stood in his way. She should be afraid of this feral side of him, and the wild look in his eyes, but for some inexplicable reason … she wasn't. In a move quicker than she anticipated Alex had her hand and was pulling her through the thick crowd. Before she could ask him what he was doing they were down a long, semi-secluded hallway where the shadows were far too thick for her comfort. He pressed her against the wall, and the coldness of it seeped right through her skin. She was breathing heavily, unable to catch her breath, and not knowing if she should surrender to the carnal look reflected on Alex's face or run in the other direction. He pressed his big body against hers, and she felt every hard length of muscle. He was still hard, and his erection dug into her belly. His face was almost stern, as if he was angry, with either her or himself. The pounding music fading away until the only thing she could hear was their combined respirations.

"Look at me, Mary. *Really* fucking look at me." His words were cold, harsh, and cut her deep, but they didn't have the effect she assumed he was going for. Instead of feeling intimidated she melted like hot butter against him. He was so controlling, so demanding, that all she could picture was surrendering herself to him. When she didn't answer he moved in so close she was sure he would put her out of her misery and kiss her, but right at the last moment when their lips would have touched he turned his head and whispered in her ear. "Tell me what you fucking see when you look at me." Mary let her eyes close as his warm breath smelling sweetly like the beer he drank brushed along her cheek.

"I…" Her mouth was suddenly so damn dry. "I don't know what you mean." Maybe if she wasn't high off of the smell and feel of Alex she might have been more conscious of what he was trying to get at, but as it stood she was putty in his hands. His chuckle was deep and low and sent all sorts of delicious tingles throughout her body, but it also sounded humorless.

"You know what I mean." The way he spoke, slowly, deliberately, had his lips lightly brushing along the shell of her ear. "You think you want me, but you don't. Not really, Mary."

Oh, she really wanted him, but maybe it was the fact he didn't really want her? But then again that didn't make any sense since she could feel exactly how much he did want her pressed against her belly. But he was a man, and she was a woman, and maybe it was simply biology and his body reacting to being so close to the opposite sex. Denying him was fruitless, and she just wanted to do this already, because the anticipation of what would happen was too much. Why on earth would she think a man as gorgeous, talented, and strong as Alex would want a too curvy, size sixteen wallflower like her? Lance had made comments about her weight, and there was no amount of exercise, even when she did force herself to go, that would make her look like the svelte blondes she had seen hanging from Alex's arms. Defeat settled inside of her, but before she could turn away from him Alex was leaning back so he could stare into her eyes.

"Do you feel how hard I am for you, Mary?" The way he said her name was so hot, so heated, that she could have had an orgasm by that alone. "Answer me." The way he phrased those two words was so dominant, like he expected compliance immediately, had her licking her lips and nodding. "No, I want to hear you say the words."

God, what was wrong with him? Did he get off on embarrassing her further?

"Yes, I feel you, Alex." Even her voice sounded weak, but she watched in surprise as he briefly closed his eyes, as if her words pained him almost.

"The way you stiffened in my arms, I knew you were about to bolt, and I should let you, but you need to know something." He opened his eyes, and they seemed more green than brown now. "Make no mistake that I want you." He emphasized his point by grinding his erection into her, which had a shocked cry leaving her. He felt so hard, so big, that she had no doubts he knew exactly how to use the heavy length between his thighs. He took his hand and slowly moved it down to rest on her hip. "Like right now I bet your pussy is soaked." His mouth was by her ear again, and the gentle, almost erotic feel of his lips against that suddenly erogenous zone lit her on fire. She *was* wet, unbelievably so, and his coarse presentation of pointing it out should have offended her, but all it did was make her want more of it. "I also know if I slipped my hand between your legs you'd let me."

He was so cocky, but so right in everything he said. Mary couldn't speak, couldn't even think clearly as he started moving his fingers in a slow glide over her hipbone. He moved it around her body so he was touching her bare back, and a surge of disappointment went through her that he hadn't followed through with what he said.

"But also don't mistake who I am." His words confused her, but that might also have something to do with the fact he was so damn close that if she leaned forward just an inch she would be kissing him. "I was going to ignore the voice in my head telling me to leave you the fuck alone, because I wanted you too fucking bad, Mary." His eyes were on her lips, and she licked them, not because she tried to attract his attention, but because everything inside of her was on autopilot now. "You're so much better than this, than me, and the fact you want me just as I want you makes this even harder." He placed his hands on either side of her head, creating a wall of thickly corded muscle. "I've fucked a lot of women, Mary. A lot." His words were like ice water being thrown on her. She snapped her eyes to his and saw steely determination in the brown/green depths. He was either being the biggest asshole imaginable, or he was trying to push her away because he really did think she was too good for him. "That's what I like to do, and that's what I'm good at. I don't do flowers and candy. I don't go home and meet the parents, and I sure as fuck don't do relationships." She flinched, but he stayed stoic. "Do you understand me?"

She did, but her mouth had suddenly gone so dry she couldn't form a word. What had she been thinking, going after him, and thinking Alex-fucking-Sheppard would give her more than one night with her?

"Yeah, you get it now." He took a small step back but still kept her caged in. "Now, if you just want a night of hard fucking, that I can give you." He let his eyes travel down her body, and she shivered from the coldness of it all. Standing in front of her wasn't the guy she had just tutored a few hours ago, or the one she met at the sandwich shop, or even the one she had wanted to desperately know. This guy was a Grade A asshole, and looked at her like she was some kind of piece of meat. "If you're looking for something more meaningful, like you're special or something, you're looking in the wrong fucking place, baby."

Her hands became fists at her sides, and her anger rose. Her whole body shook from the force of his words, from the way he made her feel like something cheap, dirty, and not worthy. She couldn't control herself, didn't even try to stop herself from uncurling her hand and lifting it to slap the shit out of him. His head cocked to the right, and she saw his jaw clench. For several long moments she did nothing but stand there, and when he turned back and looked at her, there was regret in his gaze. No fucking way was he going to feel sorry. He had already spoken his mind, and it couldn't be taken back.

"Fuck you, Alex." She shoved at his chest, and fortunately he moved away from her. Her hand stung and felt hot from the blood rushing to the surface, but her tears were hotter as they slid down her cheek. She was a damn fool, but she knew the consequences of going after a bad boy like Alex. She was just glad he had showed his true colors now. And right now her whole fucking body was covered in flames, but it was no one's fault but hers, and she deserved every painful, humiliating moment of it.
****

Alex had gone too far, he knew that with every fiber of his being, but things between him and Mary had gone from nonexistent to explosive in a matter of a week, hell, in a matter of hours if he was being honest. He had wanted her since he first saw her, and seeing her on the dance floor had his control snapping. His self-control had gone down the shitter after that, and once his hands had been on her he was fucking lost.

But then everything had gone down the shitter because she had challenged him, tried to take control, and he had wanted to show her that he was the one that held the reins. Even now he thought back to her pressed against the wall, her breathing short and fast, and her breasts right there for the taking. She would have let him touch her pussy, of that he had no doubt, but as much as he wanted her, taking her against the filthy wall at Tainted was beneath her. He also didn't want any of the cloying effects of liquor blinding her judgment.

Then something in him had snapped when she made a reference to him and the other girls, and he had known right then he had to put a stop to everything. Alex didn't have to go as far as he did, and certainly didn't have to say the things he did, but he had, and she had reacted exactly how he wanted her to. The slap was a surprise, because honestly he hadn't thought she had it in her, but he deserved it. Even now his cheek stung like a bitch.

Alex turned and watched Mary storm away. Her ass looked fucking fine as hell as she pushed through the dancing people and stopped in front of her friend. The fact she was angry at him was like gas to the already raging fire inside of him. He kept to the shadows, and even though she knew where he was, he also knew she couldn't see him. Mary and the blonde turned in his direction, and both women wore scornful scowls. He leaned against the wall and kept his gaze solely on Mary. He'd offended her, most likely made her feel like she was a whore. And although that was the last thing he thought about her, and the very last thing he wanted to make her feel like, that had been the only thing he could think of to douse this intensity that sparked between them.

The blonde looked back at Mary, but she kept her eyes on him, as if she truly could see him through the shadows. He was the worst kind of bastard, and he would have ruined her. This was for the best. He could get another tutor, but of course it wouldn't be her, and after only that one session he wanted more. Fuck, he was an idiot and needed another drink, preferably enough to have him passed out by the end of the night.

Chapter Ten

Darcy had been pissed when Mary all but dragged her out of the club, but that was the least of her worries. After they had gotten back home she had lain in bed for a good portion of the night just staring at her ceiling. God, she had been a fool to want anything to do with Alex, and she had certainly paid the price for it. He was an asshole and had made her feel so damn cheap. He was gorgeous and lethal, and everything inside of her had wanted to submit to him. Damn him for being such a good looking prick, and still causing her to want him. For hours all she had done was lie in the dark, cursing her body for still being so wet, so needy for ... *him*.

She had finally fallen asleep at four in the morning, and now it was eight and she was wide awake. She also had no idea what she was going to do. It was clear she would no longer be tutoring Alex, and after only one session she should have been grateful. If that had been his true self back at the club than she didn't want any part of that, but what if it hadn't been his real self? It was possible he said those things to push her away. She had certainly thought as much after he said them. Mary thought of that look she had seen in his eyes when they had sat side-by-side on his bed, and when they had been pressed so closely together that there hadn't been an inch between them. It hadn't just been her imagination, not when he made her feel things that no other guy had.

The sound of her cell going off had her closing her eyes. She knew who it was, and it was too damn early to talk to her mom, but if she ignored it there would just be another call in ten minutes, and then ten minutes after that. She reached out, blindly grabbed for it, and slid her finger across the screen without looking at it.

"Hi, Mom." Rubbing her hand across her face she listened for the next five minutes as her mom talked about the wedding plans *again*, and how it was only a couple of weeks away, and how she couldn't wait to meet the guy Mary was bringing.

"Mary, are you listening to me?" Her mom sounded annoyed. "I don't like the way you've been acting as of late. I don't know if it is the people you've been spending time with, you've grown disrespectful, and I won't tolerate it, young lady."

Oh man, she brought out the "young lady", which always meant she was serious.

"I meant no disrespect, Mom. I'm just tired." Mary rubbed her eyes and pushed herself up so she was resting her back on the headboard. Her head pounded, but it had nothing to do with having those two cocktails last night, and everything to do with the face she was running on a few hours of sleep and still couldn't get Alex's arrogant ass out of her head.

"You feeling all right, honey?" The irritation in her mom's voice changed to worry. The sound of china clinking together told Mary her mother was probably getting ready for afternoon tea with her socialite friends.

"Yeah, I'm fine."

Content with that answer, her mom was once again in wedding mode. "I just called to make sure you and your date will be here on Friday evening after you are finished with your classes. We will have a family dinner with Joe and Margo." Just hearing Margo's fiancé's name had her wrinkling her nose. Joe Barton was not only an attorney, but was renowned in their community as a shark in the courtroom. That wasn't a surprise to Mary, not when everyone in that circle was always out for blood it seemed. He had a very apathetic and bland personality, but Mary supposed he had to in order to deal with his very strung-tight fiancée.

"Mom, I don't think my date will be able to come." There was a beat of silence. *Wait for it. Wait for it.*

"Mary Sandra Trellis, we have already added the extra head in the order count for the wedding, and your father and I were looking forward to meeting this boy. I've already told Marlen to make an extra meal."

Good grief. He mom was always using her full name when she was trying to be stern and condescending all in the same breath.

"Mom, things come up. I can't help it if plans change, or if he has a life outside of Margo's wedding." The lie came from her easily, although Mary supposed it wasn't too much of a lie.

"We would really love it if he came, because we would really enjoy meeting the boy that you're seeing, honey. Besides, you don't want to be the only one there without a date, right?" *God.* She should have just said no, that there was no way in hell she was bringing Alex or anyone else, but she pursed her lips and went back to staring at the ceiling. Despite the fact she was royally pissed at Alex, didn't really want to see him again, and hoped his dick fell off ... okay, maybe not the last part, but still, Mary couldn't help but image the reaction they would get if she brought the tattooed bad boy with her. It would shut a lot of people up, and bring an immense amount of pleasure to her.

"I don't know, Mom, but I'll see if he can rearrange his schedule." She should have kept her mouth shut, but it was too late for that. The excitement and hopefulness in her mom's voice were evident, and even after they hung up she knew she had made a huge mistake. Alex had made it perfectly clear what he thought about her, and what he thought she was only good for, but here she was, actually contemplating still taking him with her. And all because she wanted to piss some people off and say, without actually saying it, that she didn't give a fuck what they thought? Well, clearly *she* didn't care about what she thought either because she was actually thinking about going back over and speaking with him.

Yeah, that pretty much summed it up, but in reality bringing arrogant Alex with her was a hell of a lot better than going to the damn wedding alone, or trying to talk someone else into going with her. It wasn't like she had a lot of guy friends, none really, and the ones she did know were from tutoring, and they were in relationships. Dammit, she honestly didn't know what to do, because her pride demanded she never speak or look at Alex Sheppard again, but another part of her wanted to take him because he was such a prick he would scandalize all of the people that ever made her feel like shit while growing up. But even if she was mad at him, and especially hurt for the way he treated her at the club, like she was nothing but another piece of meat he could thrust into, her body didn't give a damn and still warmed at the thought of him. She needed to get Darcy's opinion and maybe work out until she couldn't walk anymore.

After taking a shower and getting dressed she headed downstairs. Darcy was up, but barely, and that was clear by the way she was draped over the couch, one arm and leg hanging over it, a blanket thrown haphazardly on her body, and the television muted but playing some black and white movie.

"You feeling okay?" It was a stupid question given the bags under her eyes and the almost green hue to her face. Darcy had far more to drink then Mary had last night, and clearly she was feeling it this morning. Darcy cut her eyes to Mary, but other than that didn't move or speak for several long seconds.

"I feel like shit." Her voice sounded like shit, gravelly, and like she had been smoking for the last twenty years. She moved marginally, but winced and flopped back in place. "I feel like an elephant chewed me up and shit me out."

"Nice analogy." Mary stared at the TV for a moment then turned back to Darcy who was watching her. "Why don't you go back to bed?"

"I can't. My head is pounding. I feel like throwing up, and every part of me hurts." She groaned and threw an arm over her eyes. "Why did you let me drink so much?" Mary snorted, and Darcy lifted her hand and glared at her. "All right, I guess I probably wouldn't have listened, but still." That was an understatement. "Mind telling me why we had to haul ass out of there so soon? Aside from you saying something about a guy, I don't remember shit."

"You really don't remember anything I said last night?" Mary had told her about some douche-bag in the club, had even let Alex's name slip, but was surprised Darcy really didn't remember any of that.

"Everything is a bit hazy after that third A Piece of Ass."

"Piece of Ass?" Mary had just seen Darcy grab a few shots, declining when her friend offered her some, but hadn't known what they were called. The fact that was the name of the drinks had her laughing.

"Ugh, I shouldn't be talking about alcohol right now."

"Sorry."

Darcy waved her apology off, and they sat in silence for a moment. Mary saw Darcy swallow several times, and hoped she didn't throw up this early.

Darcy knew she tutored, but didn't know she was helping Alex, or that she wanted him bad enough that she would have let him take her right there in the club for anyone to see. That realization had her cheeks heating in humiliation. Maybe she was no better than the girls he was with? There had never been a time when she wanted to do something so daring, but it seemed being with Alex brought out a lot of emotions in her that were foreign. She stared at Darcy and knew if anyone could give her advice on guys it was her friend. She slouched down in her chair and took a deep breath.

"I needed to get out of there because of Alex Sheppard." Darcy put her arm down and scooted up on the couch.

"Okay. And what does the star quarterback have to do with you?" She glanced up at the ceiling as if in deep thought, and then a light bulb went off over her head. "Wait, I think I remember you mentioning a guy named Alex. You were talking about *that* Alex?" Gone was her hung-over friend, and in her place was a very curious roommate.

"Yeah. I agreed to tutor him, and we had our first session last night. We made a deal that if I tutor him he'd come with me to my sister's wedding in a few weeks." Darcy stared at her like she was lost.

"I'm confused as to why we had to leave because Alex was there and you tutor him. Did you not see the hottie with the body I was grinding with last night? He threw Dane right out of the damn water."

Mary took another deep breath. "I had to leave because I have a major thing for him, and I know he does, too." Darcy still stared at her.

"Okay, so?"

"Because we were all but having sex right against the wall for everyone to see, and then he turned into this major asshole, made me feel like some kind cheap girl, and that is why I had to get out of there." Darcy made an O face immediately after she spoke.

"He told you this? I mean called you cheap?" Darcy was far more interested in the conversation now. When Mary didn't speak fast enough Darcy said, "Just spit it out, girl." Darcy smiled broadly.

"He didn't actually call me that, but he made me feel like that. I mean he kept going on about how he's slept with all these people, and how he doesn't do relationships and stuff. He made it seem like I was trying to get with him, like marry him or something."

Darcy's eyes got as big as saucers. Before Darcy could start shooting off more questions Mary continued to talk.

"I'm sure alcohol had a lot to do with the lowered inhibitions, because I was coming onto him just as strongly as he was to me, but then everything became shitty and awkward."

"Well, shit, Mary, I mean you do know who Alex Sheppard is, right?"

Mary clenched her teeth and gave Darcy a look that she hoped meant that was a dumbass question. "Yeah, I know who he is, but what does that have to do with anything?"

Darcy sighed dramatically and threw her legs over the side of the couch. "He *does* sleep around, Mary, like *a lot*. I mean, no girl that goes after him thinks he is going to give them more than that." She moaned and clenched her head. "My head hurts so badly."

Good. Served her right for pointing out what Mary already knew. "I never said I wanted anything more than sex with him. His ego is just so damn big he clearly thought I was in love with him or something."

Darcy dropped her hand and looked at Mary again. "I'm not saying this to piss you off or make you feel worse than I'm sure you already do. I can only imagine all of the stuff he said to you that you're not telling me. I'm only saying this because I care about you, and I know you're too smart and too good to let a guy like Alex Sheppard make you feel like this. Don't think about him, don't worry about him, and move onto the next." Darcy flopped back on the couch and closed her eyes. "I feel like a steaming pile of poo." She cracked one eye open. "You're not mad that I said that, right?"

"No." Mary leaned back in the chair and sighed. "It isn't like I haven't already thought about everything you said, but I felt something different with him, ya know." She cut her eyes over to Darcy. "I mean, in the extremely ridiculous short time we spent together, and the way he looked at me, I felt like I wasn't just another piece of ass for him."

"Yeah, honey, I know. I think the female population knows what you mean. He is gorgeous, built, talented, and can have girls dropping their panties within a five mile radius with just a smile. But unless your heart is made of stone and you are prepared to only have one night, or hell, a few hours with him, it would be suicide to think you'll get anything else from him. He is no different from a lot of the pricks that walk around thinking they own the world, and like they are God's gift to women. Guys like Alex Sheppard are only after one thing, and that's sticking their dicks in a warm hole."

"You're crude."

"But honest," Darcy shot back and offered her a weak smile. "I may like having sex, Mary, but I know that if I wanted anything to do with Alex, or guys like him, he'd just chew me up and spit me out." They sat there for several silent moments before Darcy started talking again. "Why did you even offer to tutor him?"

"I didn't. He actually got my number from another guy I tutor, which happens to be his roommate." Darcy nodded. "I just thought I could use him for a little shock value at Margo's wedding."

"So *you* were using Alex?" Darcy started laughing and immediately closed her eyes and clutched her head.

"I didn't keep it a secret. I told him exactly why I wanted him to come with me. I didn't lie."

"You actually going to BitchTron's wedding?" Darcy yawned and stretched out her arms at the same time. She had heard enough about Margo when Mary bitched about her to know her sister was a pain in the ass.

"I kind of have to go to my *sister's* wedding. Besides, I'm in the damn thing."

"I can tag along, you know, cause a scene, maybe wear my transparent shirt and daisy dukes." Darcy wagged her brows, and Mary started laughing. It was nice to feel happy instead of that dreaded gloom that had lingered the whole night.

"That's tempting, but I wouldn't want to subject you to that crowd." It was Darcy's turn to start laughing.

"Thanks, I don't know if I could restrain myself from slapping a bitch anyway. But what are you going to do about the whole Alex thing?"

"What do you mean?"

Darcy threw the blanket off her lap. "I mean, are you going to still tutor him and take him, or has that ship sailed?"

Last night Mary would have said hell no, but after talking to her mom and really thinking about it she was not so sure anymore. She could always keep her end of the deal and help him pass his course, and he in turn could go with her to the wedding. They didn't have to think or even talk about the night at the club, and Mary could certainly keep the distance that was necessary. He was an asshole, only thought about sex, and didn't care who he hurt in the process. But he was also the guy she couldn't stop thinking about, not since the first time she saw him. Yeah, she really was a masochist. Could she actually still go through with this, pretend that what they had was absolutely nothing, and still keep her heart intact?

Ugh, she was an idiot for even contemplating wanting to help him, but in return he would also be helping her. She could do it, could get through the next couple of weeks and then just a few days for the wedding. After that she didn't ever need to see him again. Feeling resolved that she would push through her anger and hurt and just go over there as planned, do this tutoring, and then be gone, Mary hoped shit didn't hit the fan because of it.

Chapter Eleven

Someone had to be slamming a sledgehammer down on his skull, because no way in hell could it hurt this fucking bad unless that was the case. Alex cracked an eye open and immediately slammed it shut when the piercing, bright light that came through his window assaulted him. He took inventory of where he was, and what the fuck had happened.

His head fucking hurt, that was for damn sure, but nothing else seemed particularly painful. Trying for the whole eye-opening thing again, he shielded himself from the horrendous glare. Okay, so he was in the spare room in his house since all he could see was the nasty old floral wallpaper. This was the room he always took the girls he screwed, if he brought them back to his place at all. But how in the hell did he get back here? All he remembered was being a royal prick to Mary, finding Vince, and the two of them throwing back the shots like they were water.

"Fuck." He was on his stomach, so he pushed up on his forearms and hung his head for a moment, willing the damn room to stop spinning. He was also butt fucking naked, which wasn't his thing when he went to bed. Shit, how in the hell did he get naked? A low moan had everything in him stilling. Looking to his left, he first saw an ass covered by a thin sheet, and followed that up to the nude back with a pair of angel wings tattooed between the shoulder blades. He continued lifting his eyes until he finally stopped at the mop of wild red hair spread across the pillow.

It took him a moment, but then everything came rushing back like a bad fucking nightmare. He'd gotten totally shitfaced with Vince, that redhead he had been dancing with before he saw Mary found him again, and then he had taken her home and fucked her. Shit, he knew they had sex, but he didn't remember it. Dread and horror settled in him because he couldn't recall if he had put a condom on.

Oh hell no. He shot up in bed which only added to the massive pounding in his skull. Looking at his cock he breathed a sigh of relief when he saw the condom still on. With a curl of his lip he pulled the fucking thing off, tossed it in the trash by the nightstand, and looked over his shoulder.

"Hey." There was a moment when he didn't think she heard, but finally she moaned and rolled onto her back. Her tits swayed from her movements, and he turned away, feeling disgusted with himself. "You need to leave." He felt fucking dirty, and needed a hot as hell shower. Scrubbing his hand over his cheek he felt stubble cover his skin. His mouth tasted sour, and he tried to remember if he threw up. He had certainly drunk enough that it was possible.

When the chick beside him didn't move he said again, "Hey, you need to leave. I have shit to do." She looked up at him from her rat's nest head full of hair and narrowed her eyes.

"You asshole. Are you seriously kicking me out right now? I just got up."

Not his problem. Cracking his back and feeling his muscles protest at the movement, he searched around for his clothes. His boxer briefs and jeans were in a heap on the floor at the end of the bed, and he picked them up and quickly put them on. When he was half-dressed he turned around and looked at her. She was spread across the bed, the sheet completely gone, and her legs spread.

"Come on, how about a little morning fun?" She moved her hand down her concave belly and started playing with herself. Alex made a grunt of impatience and pointed toward the door.

"No. I told you I have shit to do."

Her lips flattened, and she pushed herself up, completely unconcerned about her nudity.

"What kind of guy turns down sex?"

"The same kind of guy that brings random chicks home to fuck." He was being a prick, but he was hung over, pissed at himself for what he had done with this girl, and even more pissed that he disrespected Mary the way he had. No amount of reasoning could make him feel differently on the latter. He had pushed her away to make her see what a douche he was, but he still felt like a prick.

"What kind of girl do you think I am?" Her voice was outraged.

"The kind that goes home with a random guy to fuck." He used the same phrase on her as he had on himself. They were the same, no matter which way they looked at it. He felt like throwing up, and he wanted her out of his house so he could do it in fucking peace. He really didn't have anything to do today, well, not anymore. After pushing Mary away he didn't have tutoring today, and aside from maybe going to the gym to work out the toxins from his body, he was going to sit his ass on the couch and do absolutely nothing. No studying. No football. No Mary. He had practice Monday, and although he wasn't playing in games until he got his grades up, his still worked out with his teammates.

"You are such a bastard." Her anger was tangible, but he wasn't in the mood for it. He scrubbed a hand over his face again, needing a shave as bad as he needed a shower.

God, he had a fucking headache. He rubbed his temples, just needing her to leave.

He heard her mumbling profanities about his manhood under her breath, but he didn't say anything because she was right. "Fuck you, Alex."

He lifted his hand, and thanked whoever had helped him out that she was finally leaving. The sound of her wrenching the bedroom door shut, and then her angry, loud footsteps proceeded her slamming of the front door. Seconds later her tires squealing out of his driveway had him breathing out in relief. He sat on the edge of the bed and rested his forehead in his hand. He needed a gallon of water and some ibuprofen. There was a knock on the door, but he didn't bother looking up.

"Yeah?" His voice was muffled, but whoever was on the other side heard him because the door creaked open.

"You like look shit run over twice." Racer's voice was amused, which further pissed off Alex. He lifted his hand and flipped him off. Racer chuckled. The smell of meat had Alex's stomach roiling.

"Fuck off, Adam." Alex mouth watered with the threat of spewing up whatever was left in his stomach, but he swallowed roughly and forced himself to keep it down. "What time is it anyway?"

"It's after one, fucker. I made some burgers if you want."

Alex clenched his teeth at the foul words. Just the thought of food had him ready to puke.

Damn he had slept half the day away, although he had no clue what time they had gotten home.

"Dude, please. Shut the fuck up about the food."

Racer chuckled again. "Well, I can make you some eggs, you know with the really runny centers. Or I can get you some slightly undercooked sausage, you know, to help settle your stomach."

Alex grabbed a pillow and chucked it at Racer.

"Fuck you, Adam."

Nausea slammed into him, and Racer laughed loudly before darting out of the room. Alex stood and quickly walked to the bathroom, threw open the lid, and puked until he started dry heaving. Well, shit, he couldn't remember the last time he had thrown up.

He flushed the toilet and stood, bracing himself on the edge of the sink. When he glanced at himself in the mirror he winced at how nasty he looked. Dark circles under his eyes, his hair standing up every which way, and the five o'clock shadow from hell. His mouth tasted stale, and every part of his body ached. He had really fucked things up with her, but it had been for the best, because her wanting him was not only like a dream fucking come true, but also bad news. In the end he would hurt her, because that was what he was good at doing. Hell, he already had hurt her.
****

Mary knew this was a bad idea as soon as she made up her mind, and that feeling of dread continued to grow when she got in her car, drove to Alex's house, and now stood at his front door waiting for someone to answer. Her heart thundered hard in her chest, and her mouth had gone dry. Her anger still simmered below the surface, and her damn arousal was making its way through her body. The front door swung open, and she was struck speechless when she saw it was Alex in nothing but a pair of loose, low hanging sweats, and a towel slung over his wide, muscular shoulders. There was that dark, delicious ink that started on his right arm and wound its way over his shoulder and disappeared to his back. She knew that the wide expanse of his back held those intricately dark lines that swirled, twisted, and were sharp in contrast to his golden, hairless skin.

"Mary? What are you doing here?" She snapped her eyes to his and felt her cheeks heat. No doubt he just caught her checking him out. The way his jaw clenched, and the dark look that crossed his face had her nervousness leaving and anger replacing it. This had been a bad idea, but she was here now, and she would make her intentions perfectly clear. He leaned against the door frame and crossed his arms over his chest. There wasn't an ounce of fat on him, and the way his abdomen clenched, showing off his six-pack, and the way his biceps bulged had instant heat pooling between her legs.

Don't get caught up by the pretty, sparkly things, Mary.

"I'm going to be perfectly honest. I am only here because I need you to still go with me to my sister's wedding. If you weren't my last resort I would have been happy to never see you again. The truth is I don't know any other males that don't have a girlfriend, or who I would even think would entertain the idea of going with me." Some of what she said was a lie, but not quite, and of course she wouldn't tell him that. He ground his teeth, but other than that he gave no outward reaction. "You're a dick, plain and simple, and I don't want anything from you aside from being my date. I'll still tutor you as long as you agree to go with me."

A beat of silence passed before he answered. "Are you serious?"

"I guarantee I wouldn't be here if I wasn't." She remembered last night, the hurtful way he made her feel, and the way he looked at her so unapologetically that her heart had twisted. "I want nothing else from you. This is just a business deal. I'll help you pass your class, and you go with me the weekend after next. When everything is said and done we can go our own ways, without having to ever think about each other again."

He didn't say anything for a long time, and with each passing second she grew more and more uncomfortable. After thinking about all of this before she left the house, she honestly hadn't thought about what she would do if he turned her away. She supposed she could just go dateless and deal with Margo and her mom, which was a lot worse than it sounded. He could appreciate a simple business deal, one that would benefit both of them, surely.

"I can always ask Adam if he wants to go with you." He cocked his eyebrow, and she curled her hands into fists. Oh, she had thought about Adam, albeit only for a moment. He may be big and muscular, but he was far too charming and nice, and no doubt would be a perfect gentleman. How sad was it that Mary wanted the complete opposite when she was around those snobs?

"Adam is too nice. I need a guy that is an asshole, knows it, and doesn't care." The dark look that covered his face had pleasure filling her. Good. She was glad she got a little reaction out of him. "I'm not holding a gun to your head. You either will or you won't, but I'm not going to stand here all day and wait for you to make up your mind." Mary was pretty proud of herself for having a steady voice and not flinching under his unwavering glare.

"For as smart as I know you are, I am surprised to see you on my doorstep."

Why was he acting like this? No, she knew, because he was a pompous fucker. The Alex she had met just last week, the nice one that smiled at her genuinely, and spoke softly to her, was not the guy standing in front of her.

"Are you in or not? I don't have time for this shit."

He lifted a dark brow at her, and the corner of his mouth twitched. Damn him for still making her want him after the way he acted, and damn him for thinking this was funny. It wasn't, and she would make a point that not all women were mindless twits when it came to him. He stepped away from the door, held it further open for her, and gestured for her to enter. Mary didn't look at him as she stepped into the house and stopped once she was in front of the stairs.

"We can do this in the kitchen." She turned, looked at him, and narrowed her eyes when the corner of his mouth twitched again. "You need to take this seriously. I'm not the one failing a course and having my football season threatened." That had his smirk vanishing and his jaw clenching.

"You came here, don't forget that. You need me as much as I need you." They were in some kind of stare off for a long while, and it was only when Adam stepped into the entryway that she looked away.

"Hey, Mary." Adam was all smiles as he stared at her.. Yeah, he blatantly checked her out on occasion, but he was a genuine guy, unlike some guys she knew. "You look nice today." Mary would have thought that was some kind of sarcastic stab at her clothing, but there was no asshole-ness coming from him.

"Thank you."

She purposefully made sure to dress in the rattiest jeans and t-shirt she had, ones reserved for cleaning the house. Adam turned his attention to Alex. "Dude, you're going to break your teeth if you grind them any harder." With that Adam sauntered out the front door, leaving the two of them alone once more.

"All right, let's just get this over with." She headed into the kitchen and started getting the books and notebook out of her backpack. Alex came in a few seconds later and went over to the fridge.

"You want something to drink?"

Without looking at him she said, "No, I'm good."

This was awkward, but she could handle an hour at a time in his presence. She sat down and focused on the things in front of him. If she didn't the smell of him freshly showered, and the sight of his ridiculously ripped chest with that defined cut V of muscle leading below his pants, would have her flustered until she couldn't form a coherent sentence. She lifted just her eyes when he bent over and reached for something in the fridge. The sight of his toned back was impressive, especially those muscles right under his arms, but that wasn't what had disgust moving through her. Three long scratch marks lined his lower back, scratch marks that a woman would have given him when he screwed her. He made his way back to her, pulled out the chair across from her, and sat down. Mary had lowered her gaze before he knew she had been staring, and pushed images of exactly what he had done last night out of her head. It wasn't her business, and what Alex did, and who he did it with, was no concern of hers.

"Listen, about last night—"

Oh, hell no. No way was he going to apologize for the shit that went down, and what, right after he fucked some girl, most likely a random one? Honestly she was glad he had said the things he had to her last night. It reminded her that Alex wasn't for her, and never would be. She held her hand up, stopping him from continuing on with that. Finding all of her strength, and not about to let him smooth things over as easily as he probably did with a lot of thing, Mary looked him in the eyes.

"There is no need for apologies, Alex." His big, wide chest rose and fell as he inhaled deeply. "I'm here to help you, and because I need your help in return. Besides, it looks like you had plenty to occupy your time last night after I left."

Why did you say that? God, she needed to learn to keep her mouth shut. She lifted her eyes to him, saw the confused expression on his face morph into one of embarrassment, anger, and what? Was that regret? He cornered her, literally and in the figurative sense. Growing up she had met a lot of people like him, ones that thought about themselves, didn't care what others felt, and had blinders on. Well no more. They had made an agreement, reached an understanding, and that was it.

"We are using each other, and that is all." She was stronger than he gave her credit for. "Now, can we just move past last night, get this over with, and then we both can forget the other existed?"

He clenched his jaw again and held his hands in tight fists on top of the table. His whole body grew taut, and his muscles flexed and bulged beneath his skin. Well good, she was glad she was pissing him off, because he deserved to be just as angry as she was.

"Wouldn't have thought you had a mouth like that on you, Mary." The way he said her name gave her chills. He looked ready to explode, like he was barely hanging on to his control. Maybe she should have been frightened, but all she did was thrust a book at him and tell him what page to turn it to. Mary forgot about everything else and started going over the material in the book. For the next hour Mary didn't make eye contact with him, but she sure as hell felt his stare all the way through her, and because of that she was even more determined to keep her distance. That was easier every time she thought about those scratches he wore.
****

Alex stared at Mary sitting on his living room floor. It had been a week since she had come to his house, surprising the shit out of him, considering the douche-bag way he acted toward her at Tainted. Her mouth was moving, but all he could concentrate on was how fucking hot she was. He still felt shame that she had seen scratch marks on his back from the night of sex he didn't even remember, and although it had been seven days since that happened, he still felt gross about it, and ashamed that he had worn the damn things like some kind of scarlet letter. Then his thoughts morphed into the night he'd had her pressed against the wall at Tainted. He could still smell her, that underlying scent of sweat mixed with the light, floral perfume she wore. He had been so fucking hard, and just thinking about it now made him harder yet. Even now, when she only wore a pair of shorts and a loose fitting t-shirt he found himself shifting on his seat, trying to alleviate his hard-on.

"Alex, are you even listening to me?" He snapped his eyes from where he had been looking: at her perfectly rounded breasts. Her attitude over the last week had been icy, but she was slowly starting to talk to him in a voice that wasn't monotone and filled with distaste.

"What?" Fuck, his damn voice cracked like he was some kind of teenager going through puberty. He cleared his throat and leaned forward so he was resting his forearms on his thighs. "I'm listening."

No, he wasn't, but she didn't need to know that. Over the last week he had caught on to the basics of what this class was really about, and knew he had been so off about the subject matter that he was actually embarrassed by the fact.

"Yeah?" She crossed her arms and arched a perfectly shaped dark eyebrow.

Shit, he really wished she wouldn't do that because all it accomplished was plumping up her breasts, and showing him a nice shot of cleavage. When he didn't answer and was finally able to tear his gaze from her chest, it was to see her blue eyes snapping with challenge. When she didn't tell him to fuck off and keep his eyes to himself, he felt a little high, and decided to see how far he could push it. It was a dumbass move on his part, seeing as she was just now starting to talk to him in a not tutorial way. He let his eyes travel down her legs, and stopped when he saw the fabric of her shorts gap at the junction of her thighs. *Fucking hell.* Rubbing his hand over his jaw he averted his eyes, knowing that he was just working himself up for no reason, and if he didn't get his arousal under control she would no doubt see the wood he was sporting.

"Yeah." He looked at her again and smirked. "You were talking about the rise of proximity in underdeveloped countries." She didn't show any reaction, and he was pretty damn proud of himself for being able to pull that answer out of his ass when his thoughts had been on much more pleasant things. He had seen her the past three days in a row, and only had one more week of tutoring before he was going with her to her sister's wedding.

Every time he saw her he found himself wanting her that much more, and each time she looked into his eyes he wanted to tell her he was sorry for the way he treated her at the club, that he had acted like an ass, but that he had tried to make a point, that he was worthless when it came to being the kind of guy a girl like her deserved. He wanted to tell her he was sorry, but every time the words came forth she would look at him, shake her head like she knew what he was going to say, and finishing talking about a subject he could care less about. He just wanted to know more about her, and found himself aching to ask her where she came from, if she had any siblings, and other things that he had never cared about when confronted with the opposite sex. He was in uncharted territory right now, and had no idea how to navigate when it came to trying to be a decent guy, and not one that was just looking for another one-night stand.

He had fucked up, and what sucked even more was the knowledge that if she hadn't come to his house, and been the bigger person, she wouldn't be sitting in front of him right now because he was too much of a stubborn asshole. He would have blocked her out, gone on with his life, and always wished he had done it differently. He only had a short time left, because he knew after his mid-terms she would want nothing to do with him, and that realization hurt like a bitch.

Chapter Twelve

"I don't know about this, Darcy." Mary held her gym bag tighter as she walked down the shady looking alley that apparently was how to get to this incredible, but secret gym owned by a former MMA fighter. Darcy looked over her shoulder and smiled.

"Of course. Mica told me how to get here." Mary swallowed and looked around. It was still daylight, but that didn't mean safety was guaranteed, especially when downtown.

Apparently Darcy and the pierced guy, Mica, she had been dancing with at Tainted had hit it off. They had been talking for the last week, sometimes several times a day. It was sickening to watch, but Mary also saw how happy Darcy was. Yeah, it may have only been a week, but Darcy went through men as fast as she did underwear. That didn't mean she looked down at her friend, because even if she might have been the equivalent of Alex when it came to being experienced in sex, she didn't have an arrogant air around her like he did. The sidewalk beneath their feet was cracked and even missing in some parts. A few dumpsters were lined up to their left, and a door slammed open right as they walked by it. A heavy set man wearing a greasy apron shuffled out with a large black trash bag slung over his shoulder. His gut protruded under the dirty material. He eyed them suggestively for a moment before he walked over to one of the dumpsters and tossed the bags into it.

This whole situation gave Mary the chills. She should have stayed home, or at least just gone to the gym she normally did by campus, but of course Darcy had talked her into coming to this great gym that only the serious trainers went to. Mary wasn't a serious trainer, though.

"I can see the place." Darcy pointed to a building a short distance away. Mary looked over her shoulder, saw their car growing more distant, and shook her head.

"Why couldn't we just drive to the front entrance?"

"Because Mica said it's a bitch getting back on the main road since it's a one-way street and they're doing construction. He said going through here is a straight shot to the facility. Besides," Darcy looked over her shoulder and grinned again, "This alley is just used for the restaurant, and a few boutiques. He told me to call him when we got here, but I don't want him thinking I need him for everything." Mary rolled her eyes.

"I don't know why you didn't since you guys talk on the phone ten times a day."

"You're being dramatic. Come on."

Ugh, she was so missing the point.

"Only girls asking for trouble go down back alleys because some guy told them it was okay."

Darcy snorted but didn't turn around. "If you pick up the pace we will get there sooner." They broke through the alley and stood right across the street from the front doors of what didn't look like a training facility.

"You sure this is the gym?"

Darcy looked both ways, then reached back and took her hand again, and all but dragged her across the street. "Yeah, I told you, unless you know about this place you would never know it was here."

"And why did you feel the need to come here because a guy you met last week said it was the place to go?" Mary also didn't point out that Darcy didn't even like exercising, and compared it to getting kicked in the crotch.

"Because I need to get rid of my muffin top, and besides." She stopped and looked Mary right in the eye, which had her stopping also. "I really like him. He isn't like the other guys." Before Mary could respond on that Darcy continued talking. "I know I've said that about others, but Mica makes me feel things that I have never felt. He makes me laugh, holds my hand instead of trying to get in my pants, and won't even have sex with me until we know each other better." That had Mary's eyebrows lifting. "I know, crazy, huh?" Darcy smiled broadly. "I really like him, Mary." They stared at each other for a moment, and Mary smiled in return. "Besides, you're always complaining about that gym you go to, how it's always crowded and the guys there are inflated to the max."

Yeah, Darcy was right. Mary didn't bother reminding Darcy, again, that she had only known Mica for a week, because her friend was elated, and who in the hell was Mary to pop her happy balloon? She looked at the building again. It looked rough. A look to her right showed construction going on, and to her left showed the busy main street. Okay, so Mica had been right about it probably being a bitch to drive right to the door, but still, that didn't make her feel any better about walking down that creepy ass alleyway, or into a building that looked shady.

Darcy was right about the gym Mary went to. It was overcrowded, filled with guys that looked like their muscles were about to explode out of their skins, and attitudes that matched a fresh pile of dog shit. She tilted her head back and stared at the tall, red brick building. It was similar to other older buildings in Columbus, with its aged look and standard box-like structure.

"All right, then, come on." Darcy pulled her forward and into the building. The air conditioning hit Mary in the face right away, but it was the sounds of men grunting, curses ringing out, and low, steady thumping of music playing overhead that drew her attention. She leaned in close and whispered into Darcy's ear.

"Are you sure women even come here?" She couldn't see the main workout room since there was a wall separating the small, front office, but the pictures hanging behind the front desk showed a lot of men posing as if they were in some kind of UFC match. A beefy man wearing a tank top glanced up from his computer screen and eyed them both. Darcy stepped forward and leaned against the counter.

"Mica recommended this place." From Mary's standpoint she could see the skeptical look on the guy's face. He was tanned, but naturally, not the fake and bake look. His dark hair was in spikes around his head, and he had what seemed to be the standard tribal-like tattoos around both of his muscular biceps.

"Mica told you to come here?"

Darcy nodded and stepped away from the counter.

"Hold up." He picked up a phone and waited before he started speaking in it. "Yo, I got two birds here saying Mica told them about Frost."

Birds? Did he seriously just call them that? After listening to whatever the person on the other end said he hung up and motioned them forward with a crook of his finger.

"Boss says you're good to go, but you need to fill out the waivers."

They each took a form, handed him their IDs to make copies, and sat down on the fold-out chairs off to the side. The waiver was similar to the one she was required to fill out at the gym she normally went to, and pretty much said if she got hurt at Frost they weren't liable for any injuries. After they finished filling the forms out he took them around back to a small door. Inside were a line of blue lockers on either side of them where they could put their things. He left them after explaining that going out the door straight ahead would lead them to the main work-out room.

"God, what was with that guy?" Mary said, which had Darcy laughing.

"I don't know, but did you hear him call us birds?" That had Mary laughing, too, and her irritation leaving. "I mean what a pig." They grabbed their towels, tightened their ponytails, and headed out. As soon as Mary stepped out into the main floor she stopped, which caused Darcy to run right into her back. She stumbled forward and looked around. This certainly wasn't like any gym she had ever been to. In the center of the room was a boxing ring. Off to the right were several punching bags that hung from the ceiling, and to the left was a line of the standard workout equipment: treadmills, weights, ellipticals, and blue mats that covered the ground. But those things weren't what had Mary realizing she was totally out of her element. She saw only one woman working out, but she was ripped beyond belief, and could easily hold her own up against the muscle that filled the room. The men were mostly shirtless, with sweat dripping down their hard bodies, and looks of steely determination on their faces. This wasn't a gym where beefed up guys came to work-out and pick up women. No, this place was for the serious fighters, the ones that were all about the art of the sport and weren't about to be screwing around with anything else.

"Darcy, I think we are totally out of our element here." She tilted her head back and saw that the place must be one huge room with a few walls dividing it.

"Have you ever seen so many hot guys in one place? And I'm not talking about the steroid injected ones that hang around at the clubs. I'm talking about the *real* ones." Darcy had a point. These guys didn't have muscles that looked grossly out of proportions. They had toned, defined bodies that you could tell they worked their asses off, and the way they looked, as if anyone fucked with them they'd kick some serious ass, made her feel wholly feminine.

"Come on, let's go to the treadmills."

They walked past the ring where two guys were boxing. Their shirts were off, sweat coated their bodies, and their concentration was only on each other. They moved with synchronized movements, seeming to know the other's position before it was even revealed. They punched, jabbed, and blocked each other's hits, and the testosterone and masculinity filled the air.

"God, I just had a series of orgasms watching them beat the crap out of each other." Yeah, Mary could totally relate. "Mica said he'd be here, but I don't see him." They stopped in front of the treadmills, and Darcy looked around. "Maybe he's in one of those rooms?"

There were a few closed doors lining one of the walls, but Mary hadn't come here to look at the man candy, although she was seriously reconsidering that. She needed a good work-out, one that would exhaust her and not have her thinking about the guy that had been consuming her thoughts for the past two weeks.

Mary picked a treadmill, not bothering to snap Darcy out of whatever trance she was in, and started the machine. She set it for a workout that would start off slow and increase in pace and incline. After a few minutes Darcy climbed onto the treadmill beside her and started her own workout. For the next five minutes they were silent, and all other sounds except Mary's feet hitting the machine, were blocked out.

For the last fourteen days she had tried her best to steer clear of Alex unless it was in the form of tutoring him. For the most part she succeeded, making herself relive that night at the club, and when she had seen the scratch marks the next morning to make her anger fresh again. It was childish to keep it up, but she feared that it would be too easy to fall into the trap of forgetting everything that had happened, and giving herself to Alex. Then there had been the times she had walked past the football field, heard the guys practicing, and found herself going over to watch him. He was a machine on the field, taking down his teammates like they were annoying flies. Keeping her emotions in check hadn't been as easy as she thought, especially when she had tutored him the last three days.

Margo's wedding was next weekend, and midterms right after that. She was determined to make sure Alex passed that class if it killed her. No way in hell would he be able to hold it against her if he failed. He was smart, more so than he gave himself credit for. He just didn't try, and that was his problem. If only he stopped staring at her, stopped letting his emotions play across his face as strongly as if he was actually telling her he wanted her then and there.

Her routine kicked into the next gear, and she ran faster. Sweat started to bead at her temples, and she reached for her earbuds and put one in each ear. Darcy was already mouthing the words to whatever song she was listening to, so Mary focused in front of her, which was of all the men working out. She turned up the volume on her iPod, and like she did every other time before let the music take her away. Closing her eyes she was washed away in the sad, heart wrenching lyrics coming from the song "Wrecking Ball". She hated and loved the song. She kept her eyes closed, listening to how deeply the song was sung, and how a part of her could relate to it. She wanted to be let in, and never wanted it to come down to this. She had walked away, but he pushed her away.

She opened her eyes and faltered slightly in running at the man who was in the middle of grappling with another, mere feet from her. All she could see was his back, but she knew that back, knew those sharp, dark lines that covered the entire muscular expanse. The song was on repeat, and she didn't stop running as she watched him wrestle with the other guy. His moves were powerful, exact, and had her whole body heating. In a move that made her knees weak he stood, grabbed the guy around the waist and around one of his legs and lifted him above his head. She didn't blink, didn't even breathe as she watched him bring the other guy down on his back, hard. It was such a display of force, of masculine power, that she swore the ground shook beneath her. Over and over they fought, Alex always getting the upper hand. Although the moves looked painful and dangerous, the men knew what they were doing, and expected each and every action and reaction.

The men broke apart when an older man, maybe in his late thirties or early forties, stepped onto the blue mats. His blond hair was in a faux hawk style, and there was no denying the raw power that he wielded. She could tell he held authority, and by the way his muscles were clearly visible through his white t-shirt and track shorts, she knew he was also deadly.

Movement to her side caught her attention, and she forced herself to look away from Alex. Mica sauntered over to them, his body sweaty, his dark hair plastered to his forehead, and his lip ring glinting under the florescent lights. His lips moved, but of course she couldn't hear what he said with music blasting in her ears. She looked over at Darcy who wore a wide grin. Darcy hopped off the treadmill and rushed over to him, like she hadn't just seen him last night, or talked to him an hour ago. Mica scooped her up like she weighed nothing, but then again he was a big guy, not as tall or muscular as Alex, but big nonetheless.

Alex.

She looked over at him again and held her breath when she saw him staring right at her. Sweat dripped down his face from his dark hair, over his wide shoulders, and down that ridiculously ripped abdomen. He didn't even bother wiping the wetness from his eyes, just continued to stare right at her. He looked dirty from fighting, was breathing hard from exertion, but the way he watched her, made him seem like he was in control of every little thing. He let his eyes travel down her body, well, as much as he could see, and she swore she saw his pupils dilate. The clothes she wore were for working out, but the pants were tight, and her top just as snug as it hugged her breasts. She should have worn something sloppy that hid her junk in the trunk, or her rounded belly.

Don't fall for it. Remember who and what he is. Those thoughts faded as quickly as they had come the longer she looked at him, and dammit she couldn't look away. Her pulse kicked into overdrive, her palms started to sweat like the rest of her body, and all she could do was think about how much she wanted him. The treadmill kicked off, and she was left standing there panting, but her increased respirations had more to do with the fact that Alex staring at her made her feel bare. She pulled out her earbuds and gripped her iPod tightly in her hand.

This was ridiculous, and her reaction to seeing him, when she had just seen him yesterday, when she was trying to practice self-restraint in all things concerning him, was bordering on insanity. She just needed to go, before she did something she regretted like going up to him, taking his face in her hands, rising on her toes, and kissing the fuck out of him. Yeah, that would be something she could never take back, and would set into motion a lot of things that could and would backfire.

Chapter Thirteen

"I think I'm done here, Darcy." Mary tore her eyes away from Alex, walked past Darcy who was still in Mica's arms, and made her way quickly to the locker room. She was letting him get to her, and to be honest this was all on her. All he did was look at her and she was a wreck, and it was like everything that had happened well … had never even occurred. She pushed the door open and leaned against the lockers. The metal was cool against her overheated skin, but it didn't help in cooling her down. Perspiration moved between her breasts and down the center of her back.

What was she doing? Playing with fire, that's what. Since the first time she saw him she had felt something deep, which had been ludicrous then and still was now.

The sound of the door opening pierced her inner musings, but she didn't bother looking up.

"I'm sorry to bail on you, Darcy. I just need to get away from him." She wasn't going to tell her roommate about what was going on inside of her, at least not until they were in the safety of their house, and away from the object of her frustration and arousal. When Darcy didn't answer she lifted her head, but it wasn't Darcy who stood a foot away from her, but Alex, and he looked pissed. Slowly she stood and faced him.

"What the fuck are you doing, Mary?"

Anger spiked inside of her at his cold tone. *That bastard.*

"I guess it's not obvious." She moved her hands up and down her body as if to show him her sweaty self. He infuriated her. First she was hot for him, not even able to think clearly, and then he opened his damn mouth and pissed her off. There had never been a person that could make her feel annoyed, angered, and aroused all in the same breath, but Alex was doing a fine ass job of it. "But I think I may be working out at a gym." Her sarcasm was thick. He didn't move, didn't blink, and damn him, showed no freaking emotion.

"You know what I mean." He was still shirtless, still sweaty, and still looking so damn delicious. He crossed his arms over his chest and stared at her. "Why are you at this place, and why in the hell are you pissed now?"

"Fuck you, Alex."

He smirked, but it held no amusement.

"I can make that fucking happen, Mary, if you just pick whether you'll forgive me, or if you still want to stay mad at me." They stared at each other for a long while, and when he realized she wasn't about to respond to what he had to say he spoke again. "How did you find out about this place anyway? This part of town isn't really safe for you to be coming to, especially alone."

Mary felt like a scolded child. She crossed her arms under her breasts and glared at him. "I'm not alone. I came with Darcy. Not that what I do is any of your damn business." She lifted her chin, pissed further that he was now trying to act like her father, like he actually cared about her and what happened in her life. He took a step closer, and she took one back.

"You mean that tiny thing out there all over Mica?" He took another step forward, and she held her hand out to stop him.

"What the hell do you think you're doing?"

He moved another step toward her until she had to place her palms against his damp chest to stop him from coming any closer.

"What do you mean?" Was he purposefully making his voice even deeper, and filled with heat? She swallowed and lifted her eyes from where her hands were on his body to his face. "If I didn't know better I'd think you're stalking me." He smirked, and she glowered. Mary dropped her hands, but he caught her wrists and put her hands back on his chest. "I've seen you watching me practice." He stayed silent for a moment, as if he wanted her to absorb that little bit of information. "You're at my house, and now I find you at the place where I work out." There was a teasing note in his voice, that asshole.

Her cheeks heated at the fact he had known she was watching him practice football, and that he thought she was following him.

"You are so damn arrogant." She didn't hide the snarl in her voice. "And if you don't back the fuck off I'll slap you again." It was an empty threat, because she wouldn't hit him again, not unless his cockiness went too far. Right now she just hoped her words had him backing off, because she couldn't get any air into her lungs.

He leaned forward, that smirk still on his face. "I deserve that slap, and many more, but you and I both know you don't want me to move away any more than I want to stop being close to you." Mary swallowed, trying to push the sudden lump that had formed in her throat down. "I am an arrogant bastard. I won't even lie about that, but you and I both know I am also honest. I have no reason to lie, Mary."

He was close to her, and the lockers were right behind her, not allowing her to escape. He was too close for comfort. She wanted to stay mad at him, but smelling his clean sweat and feeling his body heat encompass her, was doing something funny to her brain. His eyes dipped down to stare at her mouth. "You didn't want to listen to me at the club when I told you the kind of guy I am, and instead wanted to still push it. I don't know what you're trying to prove, Mary." His voice was low, and his gaze was still on her mouth. "I'm not a gentleman, Mary, have never been." He slowly looked into her eyes. "I've never treated women with the respect they deserve, but I've also never been with a woman that made me care what they thought, that made me want to put all my shit aside and actually try. Me being an asshole at Tainted was my way of trying to open your eyes to how wrong I am for you on every level."

His words had her anger slowly dissipating, stopped her frustration, and made something in her heart become heavy. After the hours of being next to him, tutoring, and fighting how she felt, she was tired, so very tired, and not wanting to fight anymore. But could she just forget everything? His intention to try to push her away might have been for the good, but the way he had gone about it was so very wrong.

"I'm sorry, Mary. I'm so fucking sorry."

She was shaking her head before he even finished. Closing her eyes, she knew that the last of her walls had crumbled, and if he kept going she'd be lost to him.

"Look at me." When she didn't obey he said it again. "Look. At. Me." His voice was harder, more demanding, and she realized there was no stopping how she felt. She opened her eyes and stared right into his. Their gazes clashed, hazel and blue ones, and she was unable to pull away from the trance he suddenly had her in. "I see the way you look at me when you don't think I'm aware." He dropped his voice an octave. "I should be paying attention to what you're teaching me, but it's hard to concentrate when I want you so fucking bad." Today his eyes were more green than brown. "As much as I know I am not good enough for you, and how I am likely to ruin you in the worst kind of way, I can't stay away. Fuck, I want you, more than I have ever wanted anything in my life, and that scares the shit out of me and pisses me off. I don't like this unsteady feeling I have when you're near, like I can't even think straight."

She parted her lips to say something, anything, but before a single word left her his mouth was on hers, taking over in every sense of the word. Mary should have pushed him away, slapped him like she had said she was going to do, or kicked him in the balls. The nerve of him thinking he could just kiss her, just take that from her without even asking. She should have done a lot of things, but she didn't do any of them, and instead melted against him.

His tongue slipped along the seam of her lips, demanding entrance, and not waiting for her acceptance before he was delving right in. The flavor of him was like nothing she had ever tasted, slightly salty form his sweat, but sweet and intoxicating. There was a spicy undertone to it, and Mary found herself moaning into his mouth.

He broke the kiss, but his lips were still pressed to hers as he said, "It's good, Mary. God, it is so fucking good."

His hands slammed down on the lockers by her head, causing the metal to vibrate behind her and echo throughout the room. She felt caged in like she did at the club, but she wouldn't let that night interfere with what was happening right now. She needed this. God, she really, really needed this. This arousal for him had been building since she had first seen him. He may not have even known she existed, but holy hell had she known exactly who he was. Then they had spent time together, and that slow burn had consumed her. Being with him and giving herself this moment to appreciate the delicious feelings he caused inside of her couldn't hurt, right?

"You like it, right, Mary? You like my hands on you, my mouth on you, and you really like this, yeah?"

He ground his erection into her belly, and a stuttered gasp left her. He was so obscene at times, but she knew it wasn't because he was trying to shock her, but because that was just who he was. He trailed his mouth down the side of her face, over her ear where he let his tongue trail along the shell, and stopped at the side of her neck, where her pulse beat frantically. He moved his hands to her shoulders and clenched his fingers around them hard, but not painfully.

"I'm so sorry, baby. The things I said, the way I made you feel ... it was wrong." He pressed closer, and she hadn't even thought that were possible, not with it feeling like every part of them was touching the other. "Do you accept my apology, Mary?" He leaned back and stared down and into her eyes.

She couldn't speak, let alone form the word "yes". So instead she just nodded. God, how could she stay mad when he sounded so sincere and genuine?

"Tell me this isn't just me feeling this." He lowered his head to the crook of her neck again and continued to lick and nip at her flesh. The light sprinkling of scruff along his jaw had her nipples tightening.

"No." She panted out that one word. He didn't pull away from her, but he did grow tense against her, and she swore he held his breath. A moment of silence passed between them before she spoke again. "It isn't just you, Alex." She licked her lips, knowing that uttering those words would forever change everything. "I want you, Alex. I want this so badly even though I shouldn't." The latter should have been kept to herself.

He groaned deeply right before he moved back to her mouth and kissed her brutally. For several long, drugging moments, all he did was fuck her mouth with his. It reminded her so much of sex by the way he thrust his tongue between her lips, and then pulled away just as suddenly. Then, because as if he wanted to make her even more crazed, and knew that he could, he started grinding his huge erection into her stomach. Over and over he did this, drawing out more wetness between her thighs and soft mewling noises from her throat.

This is wrong. This is right. She should stop him. No, she should bring him closer.

He broke the kiss, tightened his hold on her arms, and spun her around until her back was down against the smooth, ice cold wall on the other side of the room. The wall of lockers now obstructed the view of the door, and there was no doubt in her mind he had planned that. Alex pressed his erection against her belly, ground that thick, solid length into her soft flesh, and didn't let up until she realized it was all for her.

"I'm so damn sorry for making you feel less than what you are, Mary." He looked into her eyes, and she held her breath, feeling exactly how much he meant them. "I said those things, did those things, because I thought pushing you away was what was best. I'm a shitty guy, have done a shitload some things that I'm not proud of, and you could do a hell of a lot better." He had already told her this much just moments before, but she didn't stop him, because she could see an almost anguish in his expression, and knew he needed to say these things over and over again until they felt right for him.

He had this hard exterior, this bad boy persona, and talked and acted the part, but right now he was showing her that under all of that was just a boy. He hid behind that wall he erected, just like she did, but right now, when it was just the two of them, he showed her himself. He may have baggage, and a reputation that rivaled a porn star's, but he was a good guy, no matter what he said. She had judged him too quickly, and yeah, he had made her feel like shit, but even if he hadn't just told her why he had done the things he had, she had thought that might have been his true intentions.

"I want this, right now, Mary. I need you to give it to me."

Their combined breathing was ragged and labored. Could she actually so this with him, right here and right now? Shit, she really wanted to. The nod she gave him was short and fast, but he had seen it nonetheless, He dragged his teeth up and down her throat, causing a sting of pain to burst within her, but then smoothed his tongue along the sensual abuse until pleasure took the front seat. He continued to thrust his dick against her belly, and she let her head fall back until the sound of her head hitting the wall her pierced the room. Their breathing was identically erratic, and new beads of sweat covered both of their flesh, mixing together because they were pressed impossibly close. "God, I need this, Mary. Since the moment I saw you in my house that night I haven't been able to get you out of my head." He ground his cock into her once more, and a small gasp left her. He felt so big that her nipples tightened further, pressing against the tight elastic of her top, and threatening to tear right through the material.

Mary wasn't going to worry that giving into him might have been something that broke her heart in the end, because in reality she was sick of holding herself back, always following certain standards, and wanted this more than she had ever wanted any other time before. "I want this, too."

He groaned against her throat and moved his hands between their bodies to cup her breasts. Her top didn't allow for much give, and her breasts were somewhat compressed behind the fabric. He squeezed her breasts, gave a low growl, and slipped his fingers under the snug hem of it. His bare fingers skimmed her damp, overheated flesh, and a second later he was wrenching the material up and over her chest. They sprang free and shook from the force of him tearing the fabric away, but that was the last thing on her mind because his hands suddenly cupped her bare flesh and squeezed to the point of pain. There was no nervousness on her side over the fact her slightly rounded belly and wide hips were on full display. But it helped her feel confident over her size sixteen body when Alex touched her the way he did, like he couldn't get enough of her. She didn't want foreplay, didn't want touches, and didn't want to talk. All she wanted was to feel him inside of her, using all that raw power that he exuded to thrust repeatedly inside of her. No more thinking, no more questioning her actions or how she felt, Mary just decided to go for it and prayed she was making the right decision.

Reaching between them she started pushing his shorts down, needing to feel every part of him. He rested his head in the crook of her neck, his frantic breath moving across her exposed breasts. Before she effectively got his shorts passed the part of him she really needed, he placed his hand on hers, stilling her movements. "Why are you stopping?" She could hear her pulse racing in her ears, and feel it in her throat.

"Are you sure about this, baby, because once we do it can't be undone."

No fucking shit. She wished he wouldn't question it. Wasn't he the one that was just telling her he needed this to happen?

"Stop talking and just fuck me already."

Whoa, where in the hell had that come from? He half chuckled, half groaned, and suddenly his hands were off of hers. She quickly pushed his shorts the rest of the way down, and he kicked them to the side. A small cry left her when the scorching hot length of his dick touched the exposed flesh of her belly, but that wasn't the only reason the noise left her. A spark of iciness touched her skin, and when she looked down she saw why. Alex was pierced at the tip of his dick. She knew what they called that, a Prince Albert, and until this very moment she didn't know how turned on she could be by the sight. The crescent shaped barbell had to have hurt when they put it through him, but she also wondered how it felt pushing into her, and moving along her inner walls.

"Hold on, baby." He pulled away from her too quickly, and she braced her hands on the wall behind her. Everything felt hazy, but soon her mind and vision cleared enough to watch Alex move to one of the lockers, grab his wallet from inside, and take out a condom. The sight of him in nothing at all was like a kick to her stomach. Clenching her thighs together because the image had gush after gush of moisture leaving her, she mentally told him to hurry the hell up. She had never been a girl who liked a guy's butt, but holy hell on a cracker did he have a nice ass. In fact, everything on him was nice, and not one ounce of fat covered his massive, golden colored frame. He turned back around, and of course her gaze immediately zeroed in on the massive cock that jutted from him, and the silver metal adorning the head that glinted under the florescent lighting. Well shit, she wasn't surprised to see that everything on him was just as big and impressive.

He stalked forward, and really there was no other word that effectively described what he was doing. For a moment all he did was watch her, but she was transfixed by the way he stared at her, as if she was the only woman who had ever been partially nude before him. At that one moment Alex made her feel like there was no one else for him.

Without breaking eye contact he sheathed himself with the condom and stepped forward until their chests brushed together. He didn't attempt to remove her top, just made sure he had an unobstructed view of her breasts. As if he read her mind he lowered his eyes to that part of her anatomy.

"You're so fucking hot, Mary." He covered her chest with his big hands and rubbed his thumbs along the aching peaks. He did this for long, agonizing minutes, and just when she opened her mouth to tell him she couldn't handle anymore, he let go of her. But he didn't stop, and had no intentions of it, because he took hold of the waistband of her pants and pushed them, along with her panties, down in one, swift move.

She pulled one of her legs out, but before she could get the pants off the other one and kick them to the side he was gripping her ass and lifting her up the wall. Mary had no choice but to wrap her arms around his neck and her legs around his lean hips. His cock was steel against her pussy, the thick length sliding along her labia and parting them. Even through the thin layer of latex she felt the barbells of his piercing teasing every part of her. A groan spilled from her, and she was surprised by how needy sounding it was.

"You want me, Mary? You want this?" He pressed more firmly against her, and her mouth opened on a silent cry.

"You know I do, so stop being an asshole and give it to me already."

His chuckle was deep, and she couldn't understand how he could be so controlled in a situation like this. Mary felt as though she'd float away if she wasn't holding onto him. He didn't respond, and instead kept hold of her with one strong hand, and used the other to reach between their bodies and align the tip of his shaft with the opening of her body. She wasn't a virgin, but she also hadn't been intimate with anyone in over two years, and Alex was a far cry from average in size. His gaze was trained between them, and she wondered exactly how much he could see. What if someone walked in right now? It would only take a few short steps for someone to see them pressed against the wall. Surprisingly that knowledge turned her on even more.

He closed his eyes, clenched his jaw, and said, "You're so fucking wet for me, Mary."

He pushed just the tip into her, and she let her eyes close at the delicious way he stretched her. The feeling of that piercing at the tip of his erection rubbing against her, only hidden by the thin condom, inflamed her. A burning pain slammed into her as he continued to push all of those long, thick inches inside of her. God, he had to be at least nine inches long. He was also far thicker than she could comfortably take, but that wasn't enough to have her stopping this. Just as quickly as the discomfort started, came an intense pleasure right on its heels. He dug the fingers of one of his hands into her ass with bruising force, but she liked that added spark of pain, loved that it told her he was barely controlling himself.

"You're so fucking tight." His eyes were still closed, and his voice had gone guttural. Alex dropped his head back to the crook of her neck and used his free hand to grip her thigh, steadying her and keeping her stationed all in the same breath. With every thrust into her, she finally realized what it was to be claimed, and realized that she was already lost for Alex.

"It feels so good. *You* feel so good." He curled his hips into her and buried the rest of his dick in her pussy. They both let out a hard grunt of pleasure, and Mary curled her nails into his back, loving how he filled every single part of her.

"It's good, Alex. God it's good."

His breath became quicker when he started thrusting in and out of her, his heavy sack beneath his dick slapping against her ass. It was agony and ecstasy all rolled into one. The wall was rough on her back, scraping up and down as his pumping increased in intensity. He just held her tighter, just his stretch of one arm to hold her up and fuck her at the same time.

"More, Alex. God, *more*." Here she was, begging him for it harder, faster, and with only a wall separating them and more than twenty people right on the other side. She wanted to be the one to leave marks on his back from the ferocity of what they were doing. A part of her knew that once this moment was over the chances of Alex wanting her again were slim.

"I like it when you beg for it, baby."

He never stopped his steady thrusting. In and out, harder and faster, and Mary was right back there with him.

"Just feel me, Mary." His voice was a rough whisper, and when he dragged his tongue up and down her throat, growled in response to her shivering because of his wicked ministrations, she knew she wouldn't, and couldn't, stop herself from coming fast and hard.

The root of his cock rubbed along her clit, back and forth, again and again, and that tightening in her body, signaling her climax rushed to the surface and stole all sanity.

"I'm close, Alex." His name came out of her on a gasp as he thrust severely into her, hitting something deep inside that had her inner muscles clenching around him involuntarily.

"Yeah, that's fucking it. Tighten around me, make me come right along with you, baby." He was so strong, so potent, that she felt drunk in his presence, high with his cock inside of her. "Your pussy is so tight, and you feel so fucking good. I've never felt anything better, Mary." He slammed into her, pressing his body fully against hers as he continued to pump only his hips, bringing her closer and closer to coming. Her skin was chafed from the wall, and her thighs ached from how wide they were spread. He bottomed out, pulled almost all the way out until only the tip was lodged inside of her, and repeated the action over and over again. He was an animal, growling and nipping at her neck, rubbing his scruff against her already sensitive skin, and never giving her a reprieve. He moved his hand between their bodies, found her engorged, sensitive clit, and rubbed the little nub back and forth until her orgasm rushed to the surface so fast stars danced in front of her vision.

Mouth opening, and a cry bubbling up from her throat, she knew she was going to be too loud, but Alex anticipated it and slammed his hand over her mouth and pressed down. God, he was so dominating, so controlling, that her pleasure just continued to climb. Spearing her hands in his hair, she tugged on the strands. He moved his hand from her mouth and slanted his lips to hers, swallowing the last remnants of noise that came from her. With one brutal push into her Alex buried his entire length in her pussy and groaned out his orgasm against her mouth. She felt him swell further, felt the heavy pulse as he emptied himself, and found the sensation exhilarating. Alex sagged against her, his chest rising and falling, compressing hers and causing it difficult for her to breathe.

His hands clenched against her body. "That was—" The locker room door opening had both of them stilling.

"Mary, you in here?" The sound of Darcy calling out had both of them tensing.

Shit, oh shit. They looked at each other for a beat, and then she called out, "Uh, yeah, hold on. I'm fixing..." Shit, what was she fixing? "I've got to get my stuff." Alex leaned back and smirked at her, and she smacked his chest, annoyed. "It was the best I could come up with," she whispered and shrugged.

"What, ashamed of me?" he said just as low. He was teasing her, and she couldn't help but smile even if she was freaking out.

"Shh." She pushed him away and gasped when he slid out of her. A soft groan left him, and Mary bit her lip, hoping Darcy couldn't hear. "No, I'm not ashamed, but I don't want to be caught having sex with a guy in the locker room." She started adjusting her clothing as quickly as possible.

"You okay? I saw Alex and wondered how things are with you two, but then you hauled ass out of there and I got my answer." Darcy's voice didn't get any closer. When she was fully dressed, she glanced down at herself and made sure everything was where it should be, and then glanced at Alex. He was still naked and now leaning against the lockers in all his glory. He had gotten rid of the condom, but his dick was still semi-hard, and a flush of heat moved through her. Why couldn't she top staring at his piercing?

Because you've never seen anything like that in person before.

She mouthed to Alex, "Why aren't you getting dressed?" His smile widened, and he brought his finger to his mouth to gesture for her to be quiet.

"Mary?"

"I'm almost done."

"What are you doing?"

Shit. "Getting my stuff, but I had to change my … underwear." She closed her eyes and grimaced. *Underwear?* When she glanced at Alex it was to see his wolfish grin.

"Uh, underwear? What, you all sweaty from doing half an hour on the treadmill?" Darcy started laughing. Mary grabbed her bag that was haphazardly on the floor and slung it over her shoulder.

"Something like that." She walked past him, but he grabbed her hand before she turned the corner. He pulled her in close, and before she knew what he was doing his mouth was on hers and he swept his tongue in her mouth. And just like that she was wet all over again, and really did need to change her panties. He broke the kiss, and Mary leaned forward, seeking more. He gave her a lopsided grin, and her cheeks heated. *Damn him.* Mary couldn't help smiling back.

He leaned in close so his mouth was right by her ear. "I'll call you later, yeah?" Her heart stuttered, and she found herself nodding. "Good." He kissed her again, but there was no tongue, just a light press of his lips against hers. "Now, you better go or she'll come around the corner and see my goods." He tapped her on the kiss, and she made a little noise.

Before Darcy did come around the corner she left Alex standing there naked, her cheeks still hot from what they had done. "Sorry."

"Girl, what in the hell were you doing back there?" Darcy looked curious, even peeked around Mary's shoulder. Mary grabbed Darcy's arm and tried to steer her away, but Darcy dug her heels in the ground. "Wait a minute. Why in the hell did you haul ass out of there? Was it because of Alex? I thought you were just tutoring him so he'd go with you to your sister's wedding? You guys fighting again? Did that asshole make some other dick-wad comment?" Darcy's rapid-fire questions had Mary's head spinning.

"Can we talk about this at home?" Darcy's expression didn't flicker, but as she roamed her eyes up and down Mary, and that confusion slowly vanished, and in its place was a shit-eating grin.

"Oh. My. Fucking. Go—" Mary used all her strength and pulled Darcy out of the locker room, because no way in hell did she want Alex hearing whatever was about to come out of her roommate's mouth.

Chapter Fourteen

"What in the hell are you doing?" Darcy was all but laughing as Mary moved through the gym so fast she felt the fighters stopping what they were doing to watch. "I'll call you later, Mica." Darcy called out behind her. Once they were outside Mary let go of Darcy and stared at her. "Alex was in the locker room with you, wasn't he?" By the heat that covered every part of Mary, and the hundred-watt grin on Darcy's face, Mary knew her friend was aware of what she hadn't said aloud. Darcy leaned forward, and in a hushed, but excited voice said, "Oh. My. God. You slept with him, you slut." She looked around, but Mary knew she wasn't nearly done interrogating her. "Is he big? Oh, God, I bet he is. I knew he fucked you by the 'I just got screwed good and hard look' written all over your face." Darcy kept going on and on, and Mary glanced around, feeling even more humiliated.

"Shh, Darcy. You're so loud." Scrubbing a hand over her face and then up to her hair, Mary knew her face heated further when she felt her ponytail hanging lopsided. "Yeah, okay I did have sex with him." Darcy took her hand, and they started walking to the curb, but before they made it back to the alleyway and to Darcy's car the sound of the gym's front door opening stopped them.

"Can I give you girls a lift?" They turned around, and Alex walked up to them. Mary's heart immediately started pounding. He had a different pair of shorts on and a black t-shirt, but all she could picture was him naked and thrusting into her. "It's not really safe to be walking alone downtown. Mica shouldn't have let you guys come here alone. He should get his ass beat because of it." His face was a hard mask, and he tilted his head to the side and gestured for them to follow. They looked at each other, and then at Alex as he walked over to a truck parked next to the curb.

"You will give me details later, girl," Darcy whispered, and Mary couldn't help but chuckle. Of course Alex had no problem navigating through traffic and circling back around so he could park next to Darcy's car. There was a moment of awkward silence.

Mary opened the door, but Alex's deep voice stopped her.

"Mary, can I talk to you for a moment?"

Darcy cleared her throat. "I'll, uh, leave you two alone for a moment." Mary wasn't looking at Darcy, but she could hear the smile in her friend's voice. Why was the truck so freaking warm all of a sudden? Darcy gave Mary two thumbs up once she was out of the car and she prayed Alex hadn't seen it, but when she looked at him, saw his grin, she knew damn well he had.

"Your friend seems nice, although if she's seeing Mica she must be a little rebel." That she was.

Mary put a stray piece of hair behind her rear that had fallen from her ponytail. She didn't know what to say, but sure as hell wasn't going to let him see how nervous she was. When he didn't start talking she decided to just get this over with.

"What did you want to talk about?" His amusement from only seconds before was now gone, and Mary's heart raced even faster.

He looked out the window, and then after a long couple of seconds turned back to her. "I want to take you on a date." For a moment all she could do was stare at him, because as silly as it seemed, even after they had just had sex, this was so not what she thought he would be telling her.

"I mean, shit." he rubbed the back of his neck and looked out the windshield. Without looking at her again he said, "I wanted to do this right, but then, well, the whole locker room thing." His grin was back, and she felt her cheeks become fire hot. "I'm going to be honest. I've never done this before. You know, asked a girl out, not even in high school."

Oh. Wow. If that wasn't a bit unnerving and a little bizarre, but then again girls wanted from Alex what he wanted from them, and it wasn't about fancy wine glasses or easy conversation.

"A date?" She felt like a major bitch for saying that so incredulously.

"Yeah. Pretty fucking crazy, I know." His voice was void of emotion, and she knew she had offended him.

Before she stuck her foot in her mouth again she said, "I'd really like that, Alex." A flicker of surprise moved across his face, and then he was grinning. "I mean we did sleep together and all, and I'd look kind of easy if I didn't accept." When he chuckled she started to as well, thankful the mood was a little lighter.

He leaned forward and kissed her, right there, no doubt in front of Darcy. "I think I love you." He was smiling when he pulled back and she knew his words weren't in the literal sense, but that didn't stop her heart from skipping a beat. "You free tomorrow? I want to make plans before you realize you just agreed to go out with me and change your mind."

It was her turn to laugh, but it was more of the nervous variety. She hadn't gone out with a guy in years, but this wasn't just any guy.

"Yeah, I really would like to go out with you, Alex." The tension and awkwardness in the truck dissipated, and giddiness settled inside of her. Mary could

handle the truth, could handle being one of the girls who'd experienced one night in the star quarterback's bed, so to speak, but what she hadn't anticipated was the heartfelt apology Alex gave her, or the explanation of why he had acted the way he did at Tainted, or him asking her on a date after he already had her. She had braced herself for the worst, and enjoyed the best, and right now she was uncertain of what lay ahead. That scared the shit out of her. She would just have to go with the flow, and hope she didn't drown in the process.
****

Alex was nervous with a girl, and that was something he had never experienced before. He sat across from Mary at The Refectory, a restaurant that specialized in American and French cuisine. It was one he had passed on more than one occasion, but never in his life did he think he would be sitting within it on a date. What was sad was he hadn't even had anything formal to wear, not living in Columbus. So he had gone to Brooks Brothers and purchased a pair of slacks and an oxford so he looked somewhat presentable. He had worn a getup like this before, years ago, but being in Mary's presence in such an unusual setting, for him anyway, had his palms sweating and his heart racing. He felt like a damn teenager all over again.

"This place is amazing." Mary lifted her wine glass and took a sip. He followed her gaze to the high ceiling with the thick wooden beams, and down to the brick walls that surrounded them. "I've always wanted to come here, but never had someone to go with and didn't want to come alone." Her cheeks turned pink, and he couldn't help but grin. It really didn't take much to embarrass her, even if she was the one doing that to herself.

"Yeah, me, too." It wasn't really a lie, because until he had met her he hadn't cared about places like this. But once she said yes to going on a date with him, he knew he wanted to take her here. They had just finished up their meal, and now a comfortable silence settled between them.

"Did you like dinner?" She had gotten some kind of chicken and pasta dish, and on several different occasions he had found himself drawn to her eating. At times she acted so sensual about eating, and had even moaned lightly with each bite. If she had he didn't doubt her cheeks would have been in a constant state of redness.

"It was delicious." Her smile was brilliantly white, and male satisfaction filled him.

"And you're enjoying the evening?" God, why was he acting like a pussy all of the sudden? He had never felt so unsure about his actions until this very moment.

"Of course, Alex." Damn, the way she said his name was like fingers traveling along his body. Now it was his turn to blush. He leaned back in his seat and brought his beer mug to his mouth. He could still picture her opening the door when he picked her up earlier. She had looked stunning, and he didn't think he had ever used that word to describe a female, but he sure as fuck did with her. He was doing a lot of things he normally didn't do. She was wearing a strapless white dress with lacy looking flowers scattered around it, and the slight swells of her breasts gently rose above the top of the neckline. He had sported instant wood when he had first seen her. It wasn't just about how fucking hot she was, or that he felt so nervous around her, it was also about the way her smile seemed to light up the whole damn room, and how every time she turned that smile on him he felt lost.

"Alex?" He blinked a few times and realized he had been staring at her chest as his thoughts wandered. "Are you okay? You didn't answer me."

"I'm sorry, I was just thinking."

"Lost in thought, huh? Or do you mean looking at my boobs?" He chuckled for her calling him out.

Alex grinned. "What can I say? You're gorgeous, and when I'm around you I can't think clearly." He hadn't said it to embarrass her further, but once again her cheeks turned a pretty shade of pink. "You blush a lot." He took a drink of his beer and looked at her over the rim. She glanced down and started playing with her napkin.

"Yeah, it's a curse. I can't hide what I'm thinking or feeling because I turn redder than a tomato." He didn't say anything because he wanted her to look at him. When she did he leaned forward, took her hand, and brought it to his mouth to give her a light kiss on her knuckles.

"I like that I make you blush." His voice was low, and he made sure to hold her gaze with his own. He was such a sucker for her, but it felt damn good. "Tell me something about yourself that no one else knows." He kept her hand in his and stared into her eyes. They were such a pretty shade of blue, and contrasted with the darkness of her hair.

"There really isn't anything to tell. I'm a pretty boring person." He didn't believe that for one minute, not with the fire she had behind her eyes, or the way she could give as good as she could take.

"I don't believe that." She lowered her eyes, and he wished he could hear what she was thinking. "How about I start first, yeah?" She looked at him.

"All right."

"I have a sister that's your age, so three years younger than me. She started dating this guy that I hated.

I thought he was an asshole and used girls." All of a sudden he felt shame, because for all the shit he had given Reese, and the fact he had warned Kiera about him, Alex was no different. Here he was, telling her something he never told anyone else, because he didn't even fucking realize what a damn douche he truly was. "Honestly, I don't know why I am the way I am." Shit it was crazy to say this stuff aloud, especially to someone that he cared about. "I have used girls, no doubt made them feel like shit, but never thought twice about it. My sister and her boyfriend are pretty serious. I hated him for how he hurt her, and let his reputation and rumors on how he fucked a lot of girls make this toxic pool inside of me. But time went on, and they made up, and are now living together. For as much crap as I gave him, he ended up being really a stand-up guy and a hell of a lot better than me." She didn't respond, but there was no judgment in her face. "I was shitty to him, kicked his ass because he hurt my sister, but it all turned out to be this huge misunderstanding."

Shit, why did he tell her that? Why was she telling her any of this? Yeah, she knew his reputation, but actually saying aloud made it seem … real.

When the silence stretched between them he started to grow uncomfortable, thinking he may have really fucked up good by confirming what she most likely gathered from rumors.

"Although I had heard all about your exploits, I think you're a pretty great guy, bad boy reputation and all."

Her saying that meant more to him than she would ever know. Alex hung his head and actually felt his fucking cheeks heat from her compliment. Clearing his throat and forcing himself to look at her again, he was struck for the millionth time by how beautiful she was.

The light right above her was muted and cast a warm glow over her, like it was a halo and she was this fallen angel. "Enough about me. Who are you really, Mary? What's your favorite color? Do you have a favorite animal, food, or scent? I just want to know *something, anything* about you, Mary."

"I hate the color red; my favorite food is lasagna, and I love the scent of Christmas trees. I've even stockpiled the aerosol cans of that scent when they are on sale during the holidays so I can smell it year-round."

He couldn't hold back the chuckle that left him, and was pleased when she smiled. He reached across the table and gave her hand a light squeeze to urge her to continue. He wanted to know every minute thing about her.

"You really want to know the boring stuff?"

"It isn't boring stuff to me, Mary."

She twisted her fingers together, and before he could ask if he was making her nervous and uncomfortable she started talking. "I won't eat seafood unless it's in the form of a tuna fish sandwich. I also eat all of the toppings off my pizza first."

He felt his skin stretch as his smile grew wider. This was what he wanted to know, the little quirks that made her up, the little things that no one else knew unless they were really paying attention to Mary Trellis.

She took a deep breath. "I feel out of my element." That took him off guard.

"Really? Why? Do I make you nervous?" She nodded slowly. "Well that's a relief because I feel like a total wreck over here." She started laughing, and the sound speared right through his chest.

"It's just, I haven't gone out with someone in over two years, not since I left home." He lifted a brow because he was surprised as hell that she had been able to keep the guys from beating her door down. "My ex, Lance, cheated on me actually, and for a long time I didn't see myself as anything special. He was all I knew, and I let him make me feel like I wouldn't be anyone without him." He didn't speak, just let her continue, although he felt like ripping her ex-boyfriend's balls off. "I found him in bed with one of my good friends at a party."

She took her hand away, and he let it go. She needed her space, and that was fine, as long as she didn't hide herself from him. Alex realized he didn't want that, not now or ever.

"She wasn't upset over the fact, and although he apologized for it and acted like he was in the wrong, I knew him well enough to see he didn't think he betrayed me." She lifted her eyes to his. "I haven't told anyone how I felt about that, just blocked it out and pretended it went away after I started going to OSU. But I'll be honest, I deserved what he did to me in a sense."

How in the hell did she think she deserved to be betrayed?

"I let him walk all over me, talk to me any way he felt like, and what he did was kind of like karma slapping me in the face, waking me up, and showing me that letting someone do what he did to me would only ruin me in the end. So, although I was crushed, now I can look back and appreciate that things happened the way they did."

"I'm sorry he hurt you, Mary. It's a shitty thing to do to someone." His rage was a boil inside of him, growing hotter and hotter until he thought he would burn alive from it. God, what he wouldn't give for that asshole to be in front of him right now.

"Everyone knew what he was doing at that party with Brittany, but no one said a damn thing to me. They all knew they were screwing around behind my back, and not one damn person stopped me from going into that room and finding them fucking. It really showed me what kind of people they were, and how I couldn't rely on anyone but myself. They weren't really my friends, and I'm glad I found that out."

He had watched her face when she spoke, saw the pain she felt, but didn't know how to comfort her. Hell, he didn't even know what to say to make her smile again. Alex wanted to hurt those people for her, beat their asses until they were sobbing, crying out their apologies, and groveling at her feet. He could feel himself start to shake from the force of his anger, and his jaw ached from how hard as he was grinding his teeth.

"You want to know the real me, Alex?"

"Yes, Mary, I really do."

She held his eyes for a moment before speaking. "I am the kind of girl that let her alcoholic boyfriend verbally abuse her for far too long, and it was all because I was too afraid of what I would be, and how I would feel when I was alone." He opened his mouth, but she smiled sadly and shook her head, stopping what he would have said. "I'm not saying this to make you feel bad, or to gain anything. You wanted to know something about me that no one else knows, and I just told you my deepest secret, because I want you to know who the real Mary Trellis is, Alex. I used to be very weak, not sure of myself, and afraid of the unknown. I let people walk all over me growing up, and never held my head high because I thought I wasn't worth anything."

"Mary." Alex was once again at a loss for words.

"I have moved past all of that, and am now stronger because of it. Even though it took a lot of tears, I did it on my own." The waiter came by to check on them, breaking up the melancholy that filled the space between them. When he left them alone once again she said, "So, have I scared you off yet?" He loved that she was looking for humor in a situation that clearly cut her deep.

"No." He shook his head and reached out for her hand again. "You could never scare me off." Being with Mary was so different from anything he had ever done, and what he felt for her was like nothing that he had ever experienced before. There was no doubt he would not be the same with her in his life, not anymore. His pulse increased, beads of sweat dotted his temples, and he knew that there was no walking away. He wanted her now, and he would always want her, no matter what. He was falling hard for this girl, and he wasn't about to stop it from happening.

For a moment a plethora of emotion passed across her face, and he wondered if she had seen how much he wanted her, but it was gone as quickly as it had become visible. "I'm adopted, and growing up with Margo was hell in itself."

"Margo?" He liked that she was sharing all of this with him, and liked that she trusted him.

"My sister. The one getting married next weekend. She's two years older than me, and even though I was adopted as an infant and we grew up together, I never felt like I belonged. I'm not the stuffy, rich type like my family and the people they associate with."

Alex had never wanted to hit a girl, but hearing that Mary's sister had made her feel like that had a new kind of anger surfacing. In his mind, he'd just beat the shit out her ex twice. She placed her hand on her chest and stared directly into his eyes.

"I don't mean to dump so much information on you, or make you look at me any differently, because I like the way you look at me, like I'm the only girl you've ever seen."

God, she was tearing him up inside, and he didn't know what to say to wash that almost hopeless expression off her face, the one that had been brought up as she gave a piece of herself to him.

"Mary." She had once again averted her gaze from his, but he wanted those beautiful blue eyes looking right at him. When she did just that he said, "When it comes to you, there isn't any other female that I want." His expression was hard, serious. "You're it for me, Mary."

Chapter Fifteen

Alex couldn't keep his hands off of her, but that was okay, because she couldn't keep her hands off of him. After they left the restaurant all Mary could think about was being with him in the most elemental of senses. To hear Alex Sheppard tell her there was no other for him had everything else fading away, had her heart pounding like a drum in her chest, and had a sense of euphoria washing through her all at the same time. He must have seen what she wanted in her eyes because all other conversation ceased, he paid the bill, took her hand, and got back to his place faster than she knew was legal.

She had told him so much about herself, things she had never uttered to another person. Her fears when she was younger, the way Lance made her feel, hell, what he had done, all of it had been something she kept deep down inside of her, afraid to reveal it to another living person. He had let her talk, didn't judge her with looks or words, and never made her feel embarrassed or regretful opening up to him.

"You smell so good, Mary. Taste so fucking good." He took possession of her mouth again, dragging his tongue along hers, and causing so many sensations to pass through her body that left her confused. Here they were, in the cab of his truck in his driveway making out like high school teenagers. It was exhilarating. The lights were off in his house, and the fact he told her no one would be home for hours had her wanting out of this truck and in his bed now.

"Alex."

He continued to kiss her, and then moved his mouth down her neck to lick at her pulse that beat frantically right below her ear.

"Can we possibly finish this inside, on your bed?" He groaned, and she grinned. She had already sent Darcy a text saying she wouldn't be home tonight, and the response she got back was two crude designs made from numbers and symbols of a penis and vagina.

"Say that again." He cupped her breast, and she let her head fall back against the headrest.

"Say what?" Her words were short and breathy because what he was doing to her body should have been illegal.

He was doing wicked things to her nipple with his forefinger and thumb. He tweaked the tip, rubbed it between his fingers, and had the blood rushing to the surface.

"Tell me you want to be on my bed." He gently bit her neck, and a sigh of pleasure left her. It felt so good, he felt so good, and he knew just the right place to touch her that lit her up faster than pouring gasoline on an open fire.

"I want to take this upstairs to your room, where we can lie on your bed ... naked." She added the last part as a little tease, because if he could torture her with his hands and mouth, then she would do it with words.

"What you do to me." He didn't phrase it as a question, but at least he moved away from her so she could suck in a much needed lungful of air. In quick moves he was out of the truck, moved around the front and had her out and in his arms on seconds later. After a prolonged kiss, one where he had pressed her against the truck, cupped her pussy, had had her so wet she had actually ground herself on his hand to relieve the ache, they had quickly made their way inside an up to his room. A streetlight across the street came through the single window in his room and washed the room in a muted yellowish glow. They looked at each other for only a suspended moment before they clashed together, hands tearing at each other's clothes, mouths pressing together in bruising force, and sexual sounds emitting from both of them.

Once both of them were nude Alex stepped fully against her, his hardness to her softness. There wasn't a part of him that wasn't tone, ripped, and defined. He was wholly male, and she had never felt more controlled than she did when he touched her. A low rumble left him, and he flattened his tongue at the base of her throat and dragged it up slowly. She let her head fall back, closed her eyes, and didn't focus on anything except how he made her feel.

"I'm going to take my time with you, Mary. This isn't a quick fuck against the lockers at Frost." His voice was scratchy and vibrated against her neck. He cupped one bared breast, rolled the nipple between thumb and index finger, and moved to the next. He did this repeatedly while continuing to drag his tongue up and down her throat, like he was some kind of animal and marking her so there was no mistaking who she belonged to. It was a heady sensation, one that made her feel owned in the best kind of way.

He wrapped his huge arms around her, ground his erection into her belly, and then turned them so the bed hit the back of her legs. He used his upper body to push her back, and when the mattress greeted her he claimed her mouth once more. Spreading her legs so he could settle his lean hips between them, she felt the air leave her when all of his weight pressed her into the bed. After he kissed the shit out of her he placed his hands on either side of her head, and pushed himself up so his upper body no longer touched hers. Mary felt caged by him, by his strength and muscles, and by the sheer determination that she saw on his face. He reminded her of some wild animal, about to claim his prey … and she was that prey. He stared down her, and with a touch far gentler than she thought he could give her at this moment, moved his finger between her breasts. Up and down he did this, causing her flesh to pucker from the sensation. He never took his eyes from her, not even when her chest rose with so much force she grew lightheaded form lack of oxygen.. He trailed his finger lower, and as he held her gaze with his own, all she could do was wait with bated breath until he touched the part of her body that ached the most for him. When he reached her belly button Alex moved the digit around it in a slow circle, and then continued lower until he reached the top of her mound.

"I want to taste you here, Mary." He twisted his hand so he could cup her pussy, and a startled gasp left her when he pushed his middle finger into her body. "Will you let me?" Lowering his head so their faces were nearly touching he said, "I *need* to lick your pussy, Mary. I want to drag my tongue through your cunt until you come all over my face." Alex was vulgar in his description, but instead of turning her off it made her want him more. He slowly started to pump his finger in and out of her pussy, and pressed the heel of his hand on her clit at the same time. The dual sensations were explosive, and she gripped his bulging biceps and dug her nails into his arms. He hissed out, "That's it, baby. Fucking dig your nails into me, make me realize I'm not dreaming this up."

"God, Alex." No man had ever eaten her out before, and the thought of Alex sucking and licking at her had moisture seeping out of her, making Alex's finger thrusting slick with her need. She was burning alive, and there was no escape. "I want you to."

He didn't respond, just trailed his lips down her body and stopped when he got between her thighs. His warm breath brushed along her cleft, and even though she should have felt some semblance of self-consciousness that his face was so close to *that* part of her, the only thing that consumed her was unrestrained desire.

"*Ohhh.*" Neck arching, nails digging even further into his strong arms, and her breath leaving her violently, Mary stared at the ceiling when Alex ran the tip of his tongue along the opening of her body. He then moved it up her slit, circled her clit until she was thrashing her head back and forth, and dragged it back down to her opening where he slowly penetrated her.

"Fuck, I knew you'd taste like this." He took his thumbs, pulled her lips apart and started to devour her pussy with rapid, long licks, and powerful suctioning to her clit. His grunts fuelled her desire and sent shocks of vibrations to her core. She was close to coming, and he hadn't penetrated her, not really, not with the part of his body that she absolutely craved. Tensing and holding off because she didn't want this to end, Mary let of a string of short pants in the process. "Don't fight it, Mary. I want you to come so fucking badly."

It was those erotic, dirty words that were her undoing. Grabbing a handful of his hair, she tugged on the short, silky strands as her climax tore through her. Alex never once stopped licking her, and in fact added another thick finger inside of her right at the peak of her pleasure. It was intense, mind numbing, and something that she had certainly been missing.

When the tremors left her and she lay there sucking in air, Alex slipped his fingers from her still clenching pussy, moved up her body, and kissed her. His tongue tangled with hers, and the flavor of her, mixed with everything that was Alex invaded her taste buds. "You'll let me do that again sometime, baby?"

"God, yes." He chuckled and kissed her soundly, and she wasn't quite so bashful at the fact she had all but purred those two words. His erection was a living entity between her thighs, hot and hard. They looked at each other for a moment before he moved away from her, grabbed a condom from his bedside table, and rolled it down his shaft. She looked at his nightstand, hating the fact she was thinking the thoughts that were going through her head at the moment. Firm fingers gripped her chin, and Alex turned her head so she was looking at him.

"I have never had another girl in my room. You are the first and only female on my bed, and I plan on keeping it that way." Of course he would know what she was thinking, because Mary was quickly realizing that she couldn't hide anything form Alex. Whether that was a good or bad thing was still left to be decided. "Yeah, Mary?" She trusted him more than she trusted anyone before, and that comforted her but scared her all at the same time.

"Yeah." He looked pleased, and she also saw a hint of relief. He smoothed his fingers over her cheek, as if memorizing her. He took his other hand and moved it between their bodies, positioning himself at her entrance. At the feel of the thick head of his shaft breaching her opening, she didn't hold back the groan of satisfaction.

"Wrap your legs around me, Mary." She did what he wanted and crossed her feet against his lower back. A grunt left him when her moving around, trying to get into position, had another inch being pushed inside of her. He didn't tease her this time, just slowly pushed every bit of his cock into her. A mask of ecstasy washed over his face when he bottomed out inside of her. "It feels so good, Mary. You'll never know how good you feel to me." He pressed his face into the crook of her neck and inhaled deeply.

Alex started slowly thrusting in and out of her. He would pull out just enough that the crown of his dick was the only thing lodged in her pussy, and then he would push back into her. His movements were unhurried, languished. His eyes were closed, the tendons in his neck taut, and his jaw clenched. He looked so good, so male. He was going slowly for her, and she could see by the way he strained above her that he wanted to go faster, harder, like how he had taken her in the locker room.

"You don't have to hold back for me, Alex. I just want you to take me." He slowly opened his eyes, but only half way. The drugged look that he wore had her pussy clenching around his length, which caused him to groan deep in his throat.

"I do, Mary, I really do have to hold back. You have no idea what I want to do to you, how I want to touch you, kiss you, and how hard I want *fuck* you." He shoved deep inside of her, and she moved up the bed an inch. His hands were on the bed beside her head, and she could see out of the corner of her eyes the way he pulled at the sheets, clenching the material in his big fists. When he dipped his head and ran the tip of his nose along the shell of her ear, Mary shivered in response. "You'd run screaming if you knew how much I want to own your body, and mark you so every fucking guy knows that you're mine."

He pulled out and thrust hard into her again. She moved up the bed one more inch, and a cry of pleasure left her. He gripped a chunk of her hair, tilted her head back as far as it would go, baring her throat to him completely, and gently bit the side of her neck.

"Does that scare you, Mary?" He pumped into her again, shallowly so that she was aching for more. "Does it scare you to know that I want every part of you, and that if another guy looks at you the wrong way, talks to you, or God help him, touches you, I'll fucking beat his ass so bad he won't be able to walk right ever again?" His words were dangerous and low. "Answer me, baby." Another hard shove into her and she was forced to tighten her fingers on his massive biceps and hold on.

"N-no, it doesn't frighten me, Alex." On the contrary, it turned her on so damn much that she no longer had her legs around his waist, but had her feet braced on the mattress and was lifting her hips in time with his powerful pumping.

"*Christ*, Mary." He started moving faster, and right when she would have come he pulled out. For a moment Mary was stunned speechless. Had he really just stopped when she was so close? She lifted her head to stare at him from between her legs. Alex was on his knees, his erection jutting forward, and the indentation of the piercing at the tip of his shaft visible through the condom. He gripped the root of his shaft, breathed in and out heavily, and stared at her pussy.

"I want to take you from behind, Mary." He lifted only his eyes to her, and she licked her lips and nodded. He didn't smile, didn't move, and just continued to stare at her. Mary moved so she was on her hands and knees, and looked at Alex from over her shoulder. He still gripped himself, but now he took his free hand and ran it over his mouth, back and forth, as he stared at her ass. "Pull your ass apart, Mary. Let me see what's mine."

Her heart was beating double time, and the fact he had spoken so demandingly had her doing exactly what he said. She reached behind her, gripped the mounds and spread them. He groaned deep in his throat. He moved closer, so close that his body heat made her feel like a fire surrounded her. Placing the tip of his erection at the opening of her pussy once more, she expected him to slam inside of her, but he didn't, and instead held onto her waist, grunted, and moved back into her with a tenderness that startled her. Over and over he pulled out and pushed back in, never increasing his speed, but making sure to fill her completely and thoroughly. She ached for more, needed it as fierce as she knew he could give. The sheets were bunched in her hands, and she looked over her shoulder once more, not afraid to ask him what she really wanted.

"Alex." Her voice was soft, but strained from the need to come desperately. "I need you to give it to me. You're holding back." He looked at her, and she saw the way his throat worked when he swallowed. He was nearly out of her body, but after she said what she wanted he curled his fingers into her waist and shoved back into her, hard. "Oh, God." She closed her eyes as a ripple passed through her. He did it again and again, keeping a bruising grip on her as he pounded into her already deliciously sore pussy. She was so close to getting off, but before she could take matters into her own hands and touch herself, Alex had his finger between her thighs and rubbed her clit. He pinched the swollen tissue hard enough that her eyes watered and her orgasm crashed into her. It was agony and ecstasy all rolled into one. She bit her lip, feeling him touch the hidden, engorged bundle of nerves deep within her and felt her pleasure peaking to a volcanic level.

The tangy, metallic flavor of blood filled her mouth, but she didn't care that she had broken skin, because what Alex was doing to her at this moment couldn't be called anything but fucking her raw. Her breasts shook from the force of his thrusts, and the sound of their damp skin slapping together filled her ears. He grunted and growled behind her like some kind of feral animal, but all that accomplished was having another series of smaller contractions going off inside of her, milking him like a fiend. With one ear-splitting groan he buried the full length of his dick inside of her and came. She felt how tense he was, how hard and bunched his muscles were as he strained behind her. When his body was no longer taut he covered her back with his chest, his warm, humid breath coasting along her nape.

They fell to the side at the same time, and Alex immediately curled his arms around her and brought her back to his solid chest. His shaft softened inside of her, but was no way flaccid, and she wiggled against him. He nipped her earlobe and groaned. "You better stop doing that, or we will be going round two." He kissed her ear and pulled out of her, much to her disappointment. He left the room, presumably to go to the bathroom, but she was too tired to open her eyes and check. A few minutes later he was back and sliding into bed beside her, resuming the spooning position with her back to his chest. They were quiet for several moments, and just as she was about to pass out his deep voice pierced the stillness.

"Thank you for sharing a part of yourself with me tonight. It means the world that you trusted me." He buried his face in her hair and inhaled.

"I'm glad I told you, too." And she was. As the silence once again descended upon them, Mary let her thoughts take over for just a moment, and let herself entertain the idea that she could easily fall in love with Alex Sheppard.

Chapter Sixteen

Sweat fell into the Alex's eyes as he made another lap around the field. He may not be able to play in any games until all this shit was sorted out, but he still went to practice with the rest of the team. Alex was actually grasping what Mary was teaching him, which surprised the hell out of him since concentrating while around her was pretty fucking hard. What he knew for sure, he had no idea what the hell he had signed up for when he decided to take a Human Sexuality class. She was patient with him, because ever since their relationship had gotten physical he hadn't been able to keep his hands off of her. But her little "rewards" if he paid attention and stopped manhandling the tutor were incentive enough for him to actually focus.

Now it was Friday, and they were supposed to head to her family's place for dinner tonight. The whole situation was crazy, unpredictable, and he loved ever fucking minute of it.

He made one more lap and stopped when he reached his teammates. They all breathed out heavily, but running around the field was punishment for a few of the guys coming in late and hungover or still partially drunk.

"I should make you guys do another twenty laps just for the hell of it." Coach stopped in front of them and scowled. Yeah, he was pissed, and whenever Coach was angry it was a pretty scary thing to see. "I don't know how many times I've warned you about coming to practice hungover, but I'm sick of it. I don't care if it wasn't all of you, because we are a team, and when one of you screws up, the whole lot of you do." He scanned his eyes over the players and stopped on Alex longer than the rest. "I'm surprised more of you aren't failing your courses and in Sheppard's position. In fact, I thought you would have been smarter than he was and taken his screw-up as a life lesson."

Alex tensed in anger for being called out in front of everyone, but he kept his mouth shut. A few of the guys cast him a wary glance, but quickly averted their eyes when he narrowed his at them.

"No one is leaving practice until every single one of you sweats out the alcohol, and the only thing you'll want to do on a Friday night is ice your muscles."

There was a collective groan. Alex looked at his watch. He was supposed to head home, pack a weekend bag, and pick Mary up at her house in an hour. They would then head over to her parents'. He had reserved a hotel room, and the thought of having her all alone, under him, and crying out his name, had him hard as fuck. He adjusted himself through his outfit and walked over to where Coach was talking to a few of his teammates.

"Now get your asses back on the field and run Play 3 again until it's right." Coach turned to Alex.

"Coach, I'm supposed to be heading out this weekend with my girl. I can't really stay late tonight." There was a moment of silence. Coach shook his head. "You are one of the ones that needs to stay, Sheppard."

"I've been on time since you told me about bringing my average up, and I haven't come to practice hangover. I'm also working my ass off trying to get my grades up."

"You want an award, Sheppard?" Alex gritted his teeth and tightened his hands into fists. Coach was to be respected, but that didn't mean he liked people talking down to him.

"No, but I am telling you I need to leave. I've got plans."

Coach's expression stayed bland. "Looks like you're going to have to be late, Sheppard. Now go with the team and practice." He didn't give Alex time to comment, because he was already making his way to the field. Alex turned around and watched his teammates get in formation to practice a play. *Shit.* He could leave, but there would no doubt be serious repercussions involved, and he was already on probation.

"Fuck." He quickly walked over to his duffle and grabbed his cell from inside. After he dialed Mary's number he turned away from the field and braced his arm on the cement wall.

"Hi." The smile in her voice was contagious, and he found himself smiling in return.

"Hey, baby."

"Are you on your way?" He voice was soft, melodic, and had him closing his eyes and savoring it. Shit, he was so into her, and he didn't care what anyone said about that.

"Aww, baby, I have to stay late for practice tonight. Coach is really being hard on the guys coming in hungover." He heard the sound of a zipper being closed and knew she was getting ready.

"Really?" Her disappointment was clear. "You can't leave early? Maybe tell your coach you have plans?"

"I'm sorry, baby, but I'm already on probation because of my grades, and I really don't want to piss anyone else off."

"Well, you are still coming, though, right?"

Things with them were so different now, and he couldn't even explain it rationally. Just a few short weeks ago he would have never thought he would ache just to see Mary's face, just to hear her voice, and to touch her skin. But all of that changed when she gave herself to him at Frost's and only continued to change for the better every time he saw her, hell, every time he spoke with her.

They may not have sat down and discussed what kind of relationship they were in, but there wasn't anyone else for him. Besides, the way she looked at him told Alex she was just as into this as he was. He didn't look at other girls, didn't think about other girls, and sure as hell didn't get wood when one of them in a short skirt brushed by him. All he wanted anymore was a certain dark haired girl with vibrant blue eyes and a passion inside of her that could bring him to his knees in more ways than one. He looked at the dull porous grey wall in front of him and flattened his hand on the rough surface.

Could he actually love someone in such a short amount of time? He had never been in love, didn't know what it felt like, but the emotions inside of him every time he looked at Mary told him what he felt for her wasn't just desire for her. He cared about her, so fucking much. If this was what love felt like, this deep need to protect her, and the possessiveness that consumed him when he was around her, then yeah, he loved her, so damn much.

"I don't know how late I'll be, but yeah, baby, I wouldn't miss it for the world." And he wouldn't, because he would go anywhere with her, do anything for her, and there wasn't anything on the planet that could stop him. His friends would call him pussy-whipped, but it was so much more than that. He was in love for the first time in his life, and there wasn't anything that could take that elation from him.

****

Mary dreaded going to this wedding. Not only was Alex still practicing and not coming until later, but she was stuck in her parents' stuffy dining room having to listen to Margo going on and on about how unhappy she was about every little aspect of the wedding décor, the dresses, even the music. Of course Margo was very high maintenance, but she could also be a mega-bitch on the best of days. So here she was, sitting at the table with her family, and listening to Margo complain about how the red wine was too dry for her liking. Joe sat beside Margo like the proper gentleman, agreeing with everything she said.

"Mary, did you hear what your sister asked you?" Mary looked over at her mom, realizing she had been zoning off.

"I'm sorry, no. I was lost in thought." When she was around her family she was expected to be the proper daughter of the Trellis's. Her back was straight, her hands neatly folded in her lap, and she felt like a total imposter. It was all automatic.

"I asked what happened to your date? Did he bail?"

She glared at Margo.

"He'll be here later. He had practice, and it ran late." Before Margo could spit back a smart-assed comment, which Mary knew was poised on the tip of her tongue, the front door bell chimed, and her mother clapped.

"Oh, Mary, I forgot to tell you I ran into an old friend of yours a few weeks back." Mary's heart picked up speed because she could imagine exactly which "friend" her mother was referring to, especially since Lance had called her a couple of weeks ago. Her mom was up and moving to the door before the Trellis family "help" could get to it first. God, her mom was overly excited. She heard excited chatter and then Lance's deep, snobby voice. Moments later her mother and ex-boyfriend came back into the dining room, but Mary refused to make eye contact with him. This whole situation was bullshit. She was angry that her mom had brought him here, but in her defense Mary hadn't told anyone why they had broken up, or all the horrible things he had done to her. After their conversation on the phone several weeks back, she thought Lance would have taken the hint she wanted nothing to do with him. Clearly that wasn't the case at all.

"Mary, are you even going to say hello to Lance?"

Clenching her hands around the linen napkin on her lap, she lifted her head and looked at the guy who had made her feel like she was nothing in every sense of the word. Lance Marten, with his perfectly styled short blond hair and clear blue eyes, looked exactly how she remembered when she left him at that party two years ago. At just a glance he seemed like a perfect boy-next-door type, but under that exterior he was worthless. The argyle print sweater vest he wore was wrinkle free and flat against his starched white button-down shirt, and his Dockers were pressed to perfection. He smiled at her, but she knew Lance well enough to see a pile of shit when it was right in front of her.

"It is so good to see you again, Mary. It has been so long." He moved around the table, and she tensed. His smile was bright white and straight. No doubt he had bought himself a set of veneers. Before she could move he gripped her under the arms and hauled her up smoothly.. He pulled her close to him, and she nearly gagged at the strong smell of his Polo cologne. It was the same cologne he wore when they had been dating, and a scent she couldn't stomach any longer because she always attributed it to his drunken outbursts, and the way she had felt with him … dependent and needy.

Whispering so only she could hear Lance said, "Since you didn't want to see me on your own, I was lucky enough to run into your mother at the country club. Strange how things work out like that, huh?" *Yeah, how convenient.* "It is so good to see you." He moved back and smiled broadly at her. "I can't believe it. You haven't changed at all."

She wanted to push him away, to tell him it was only two years, not a decade, since they had last seen each other. Being in front of him again told her two things: she still hated him, and as much as she had grown since being away, and become stronger, there was still a part of her that felt small when in his presence. Here she had thought she had grown since leaving Brentsville, Lance, and her family's strict, tight rein on her life. Had she been that wrong, or was she just letting Lance control a part of her that he had no claim over?

What she wanted was Alex, to feel his strong hands holding, his scent washing away Lance's sickly sweet cologne. Alex didn't care about a title, or a social status. Her mother was all but beaming at their reunion, and her father stared stoically at them.

For the next hour and a half Mary's mom incorporated Lance into any and all conversations that were started. Mary's anger was slowly rising with each passing moment.

"So Lance, how are things with your father? I heard you'll be starting your internship with his company soon?"

Lance spent the next hour gushing about himself. Mary couldn't stand it.

"Lance." Everyone turned and looked at her. "How *is* Brittany anyway?" There was a beat of silence as he stared at her. There was no missing the way he gritted his teeth. *Aww, so a sore subject. Good.* He cleared his throat, looked between her mother and father, and gave them a saccharine smile.

"Actually, Brittany and I have parted ways." The way he said it, with a slight undertone of distaste, had Mary wondering what her one-time friend had done to him. It was clear he was pissed about how things ended with them. Maybe Brittany had gotten a taste of who Lance Marten really was and had booked it? Not that she wished ill on anyone, but karma and all that.

Lance, with his smooth talking skills, glossed over the Brittany question. "Mary, I was thinking maybe we could get together after the wedding."

Either her family was too dense to have seen the little ticks of Lance's anger, or they just didn't care to continue onto at path of conversation. "Oh, Mary, doesn't that sound lovely?" Her mother gushed at what Lance said. "I never did understand why you guys broke up, but two years is enough time to get things sorted out. Besides, you're single, and so is he."

Mary didn't correct her mother on the fact she didn't consider herself single. She and Alex may not have talked about what their relationship was, but she cared for him, and couldn't see herself with another guy. She just wanted Alex.

She snapped her eyes at her mom, but she was practically fawning over Lance from across the table. "You two should go to the wedding together." Her mom looked over at Mary. "Since your date obviously isn't coming, I think it is the perfect timing that I ran into Lance at the club."

Yeah, perfect timing. Enter sarcasm.

"I don't think so, and my date, Alex, will be accompanying me. He just had things to do, like I said earlier." She kept her face firm as she looked at her mom. She would not back down on this. This was going too far, and she had stepped right into it by not saying something sooner. "Sorry, Lance, but I'm sure you can find another date." Satisfaction filled her when a spark of fire snapped behind his eyes, and she knew he had hit a nerve.

"Well, that's a shame, but you'll save me a dance at the wedding, right?" God, she just wanted out of this uncomfortable nightmare.

She didn't bother responding to his question. "Listen, I've got to go." Mary had enough, and just wanted to get back to the hotel room and wait for Alex. She looked at her phone, and wondered where he was. As it was she didn't want him over here, because subjecting him to this would be cruel. Margo was giving her the stink eye, and her mother and father were looking at her disapprovingly, most likely because of her "attitude". In just these last two years she had really felt like she had grown as a person and an adult. She supposed when bad things happened to someone in their life it could make them a stronger person in the long run. She knew if not for the situation with Lance, and the way she had let others make her feel like shit while growing up, Mary might never have had the courage to lay it all out for them right now. Before they could stop her she stood and grabbed her purse.

"Mary, you're just going to leave without even finishing dinner?" Her mother stood, the surprise clear in her voice.

Mary turned to leave. "I've had a long day, so I'd rather just go to the hotel."

"Hotel?" Her mom's voice squeaked with shock. Mary's back was to the table, and she closed her eyes. Yeah, she hadn't gotten around to telling them she was staying with Alex at the hotel. Turning around she was confronted with everyone now standing, staring at her. There was a bit of hurt on her mom's face, and that made Mary feel even worse.

"Yeah, I thought it might be a little crowded with Margo and Joe staying here, and besides, it might be uncomfortable for Alex to stay in a place he isn't familiar with."

"Alex? You mean the 'boyfriend' that isn't here?" It was clear in Margo's voice that she thought there was no Alex. Mary was exhausted mentally and physically, and was ready to go.

"Yeah." She clenched her teeth, feeling that weakness she had always felt slowly start to dissipate. "In fact, leaving is sounding better by the second."

"Mary, I don't know what has gotten into you, but your behavior is very rude and unacceptable." Her father took a napkin and wiped the corner of his mouth.

"I agree, Mary. You never act like this. Is there something else bothering you?" Her mom had a tight grip on her linen napkin.

"Just let her go, Mother. She's ruining dinner anyway. She'll probably throw a temper tantrum at *my* wedding also." Margo sat down and flipped her hair over her shoulder.

That was it. Something inside of Mary snapped. All that weakness they made her feel, the way she allowed everyone to walk all over her and dictate her life, was past the breaking point. She was a grown ass adult, had been surviving without them for the last two years, and was stronger than they gave her credit for. The fighter inside of her rose. Spearing Margo with an angry look had her sister's eyes widening a fraction. Oh yes, no more standing back and letting herself be looked down upon.

"You are such a bitch, Margo." The room went deathly quiet after Mary spoke those words. Everyone looked scandalized by her crass statement. It felt fucking great.

"Mary—" Her mother's high-pitched voice couldn't sway her from continuing. No, this was a long time in coming.

"No, Mom, I've had enough of her shit, and of you two looking at me like everything I do is not up to par with the perfect little lives in this community." She stared at her parents. "I'm sick of always feeling like I am not as worthy as everyone else."

"Mary, honey, I didn't know you felt this way. Her mother's eyes were big and her tone sincere.

"That's because you never asked, Mom." There had been far too many times to count in her life when her parents and sister had made comments about what they expected of her, that she should wear certain things, talk a certain way, or act the way they wanted her to. She was always on display and always felt as though she never did anything right. And it had taken her this long to grow comfortable in her skin. It had taken two years to realize that she was worth something. Alex made her feel special, didn't expect her to be someone she wasn't, and cared about what she had to say. He made her feel like a human being. He may not realize it, but he had helped her realize a lot in the very short amount of time they had spent together. She felt like she could be herself with him, and that was very freeing.

The room was still quiet, and she didn't break her stare from Margo. "I'm tired of you treating me like I'm not good enough for anything. I'm tired of you acting like you're better than me. And I'm really fucking tired of you being a bitch all the time."

Her mother gasped, and Margo opened her mouth in shock, but nothing came out. Everyone else stayed silent. At least they were smart in that sense because she was feeling a fire burn inside of her and would unleash it on everyone.

"You're not better than anyone else, Margo." She lowered her voice. "You're my sister, whether the same blood flows through our veins or not. It doesn't matter to me where you come from, how much money you have, or who your friends are." She turned to her mom then. "I'm not a doll, Mom, and you can't make me act a certain way, or do certain things. I'm a human, your daughter, and I'm sick of never being able to feel like myself when I come home." They held each other's eyes for a second. In a softer voice Mary said, "And I will never be getting back with Lance." Mary held her hand up when her mom was about to speak. "Let me finish." For the first time Marsha Trellis actually *looked* at her. "You want to know why I will never be with Lance again?" She looked at her ex, saw the way his nostrils flared, and his eyes narrowed. "He cheated on me with Brittany, you know, the girl that I used to be friends with. Yeah, I caught them having sex at one of those posh wine parties they always liked to throw."

"Mary, I think that is enough." Lance gritted out through her teeth, but she wasn't about to shut up. Not now, and certainly not ever.

"It's not enough, Lance, because I want them to know exactly the type of person you are." His face started to turn a shade of red from his anger.

"You're making a mistake, Mar—"

"Let her finish, boy."

Mary snapped her eyes to her father, surprised at the low warning in his voice.

Her father looked at her and nodded for her to continue. "You hurt me, Lance." Her voice was soft, but she knew everyone in that room heard her nonetheless. "And the entire time we were dating I put up with your drunken verbal abuse because I was scared about being alone."

She would not cry even though she felt tears prick behind her eyes. They weren't sad tears, surprisingly, but ones that made her feel clean and happy, because finally getting this off her chest was like a weight being lifted from her shoulders.

"The only thing I am glad about that came from our relationship was the fact I learned a lot about myself and my self-worth by being with you. I'm different now, as you can all see, and that is a good thing." She took a step back and addressed the room. "Being on my own, standing on my own two feet and handling things myself has made me not feel dependent on others, or what they think about me. I might live in an old, rundown house with a roommate, not able to buy designer clothes or have the newest possessions, but I wouldn't trade that for anything." The tears she had tried so hard to hold in spilled free, but she didn't care. It felt good to cry, because for once in her life they weren't because she was sad.

The only sound that could be heard after she spoke was the grandfather clock in the foyer chiming the hour. "Mary, honey." Mary shook her head and smiled at her mom.

"I don't want an apology, because what's done is done. I was tired of having all of that bottled up, but it's out in the open now, and just know that I will not ever keep it in again. I owe a part of that to Alex, because he has never made me feel awkward in my skin, and has always let me know I am worth something more. I have to go, but I'll be at the salon tomorrow, Margo." She didn't wait for anyone else to reply, just headed to the front door, but stopped when she heard her father's deep voice.

"You did that to my daughter?" Mary was surprised to hear the unrestrained anger in her dad's words. There had only been a few times when she had seen or heard her father upset, and they had all been when there was an issue with work. He was stoic, apathetic on the best of days, and showed her, as well as everyone else, very little affection. It was who he was, but right now he was speaking to Lance with rage laced in his voice.

Lance cleared his throat. "Sir—"

"You are no longer welcome in my home, or in the company of my family. I want you out of here."

She heard her mother start to cry. Mary opened the door and headed out, but stopped when she saw the downpour. *Of course.* Taking her keys out of her purse, she grabbed her phone in the process, and saw a few missed calls from Alex and texts saying he was sorry he was running so late and that he was on his way. She sent a quick text to him saying to just meet her at the hotel. She was glad he hadn't gone with her tonight, because no way would she have wanted him to see that circus act. Hitting the unlock button on her keychain she took a step off the landing and made her way quickly to her car. The rain pelted her and she was instantly soaked, but before she climbed in her car she heard the front door open and close and turned around to see Lance walking briskly toward her. He stopped right in front of her, water dripping from his once perfectly done hair, and his eyes narrowed into slits.

"You made me look like a damn fool in there." She didn't miss the way he clenched and unclenched his fists at his sides. She tightened her hold on her keys, refusing to be intimidated. He wouldn't dare hit her, although she saw in his eyes that he had the urge to.

"I said the truth. If the truth makes you look like a fool then maybe you should take a good look in the mirror, Lance." It wasn't a question, but her words clearly pissed him off more because he bared his teeth at her. He lifted his hand, and for a split second she actually thought he *would* hit her. He held his hand in the air, and she looked between him and his fist.

"If you're going to do it, then do it." There was no fear in her words. Holding his gaze, she challenged him to hit her and prove exactly how weak he was. His nostrils flared, and for several seconds he did nothing but stare at her. He dropped his hand and grinned at her. It wasn't sweet and genuine, but like a damn predator about to attack its dinner.

"You'll regret doing that, Mary. You have clearly forgotten your place." With that he stalked to his Porsche, climbed in, and sped off, tires squealing and water spraying everywhere. There was the Lance she remembered, the one with the short fuse but that could put on an act to fool the Pope. Her phone vibrated, and she saw it was a text from Alex.

Alex: K, but R U all right?

Mary breathed out, feeling so overwhelmed.

Yeah, just family drama. I'll C U there.

Tossing her phone in the passenger seat she made her way to the hotel, feeling good about getting everything out, but also feeling extremely exhausted because of it. At least her family hadn't tried to stop her from leaving. Despite telling herself not to, the tears she had been holding in spilled down her cheeks.

Chapter Seventeen

Alex stood under the awning at the small hotel in the posh suburb right outside of Brentsville. They had stayed several more hours for practice. His body was sore, and after running home and taking a quick shower and packing his bag, he had headed right over. He tried calling Mary to tell her he was on his way, but there hadn't been an answer. He felt like shit for bailing on her, and even felt more like a douche when she sent him a text when he was on his way saying to just meet at the hotel. He spotted her BMW pull to a stop under the awning, and right when she got out the valet rushed over to her. She handed him her keys, and he drove the car away, and then it was just her standing a few feet from him, soaking wet, and her eyes red from clearly crying. His heart beat double-time and he moved toward her. Had those assholes hurt her? If so he'd kick some serious ass.

She met him halfway, stopped when she stood right in front of him, and before he could ask her what happened she had her arms wrapped around his neck and had her mouth on his. Surprise filled him at her assertiveness. Had he been wrong that she was upset? He grew instantly hard when she slid her tongue along his bottom lip. Alex didn't question what she was doing, just wrapped his arms around her waist, pulled her close to his body so he was holding her weight and her feet dangled above the ground, and took her mouth in a fast, passion-filled kiss. For several long seconds they stood there, kissing like no one was watching, and it was so fucking hot.

She broke the kiss, trailed her lips along his jaw, and whispered in his ear. "Take me to our room, Alex. I need to be with you right now."

She leaned back and looked into his eyes, and there was no fucking way he was going to question what in the hell was happening. Alex set her on her feet, took her hand in his, and led her past the front desk, and into the elevator. Pressing her against the mirrored wall, he took her mouth again, feeling the elevator ascend, and loving that if he wanted to he could have her right here, right now. She pressed against him, rubbed her body along the length of his, and seemed almost desperate for his touch. His pulse beat at the head of his cock, and he knew he'd need to stop or he'd pull her skirt up and take her right here in the elevator. She was wet, as if she had been standing in the rain, and he broke the kiss and looked down at her. Her dark hair seemed even darker now that it was wet, and a glance down at her chest showed the thin material plastered to her breasts, and her nipples rock hard through the bodice.

"You're soaked." He slowly lifted his eyes to hers, and his breath halted at the raw look she gave him.

"You have no idea, Alex." The way she said it made it clear she wasn't taking about her wet clothes and hair. *Holy fucking shit*. His girl was hot. Fortunately the elevator dinged when it reached their floor because he had been seconds away from taking her. He took her hand again and moved them quickly down the hall to their room. Once the door was opened and closed behind them, they stood there facing each other. The living arousal that bounced between them had his cock throbbing. He went to her, and at the same time they started tearing clothes away until they were pressed naked against each other. This was not a slow night of making love, but fast and fierce.

He took her to the bed, ran his finger between her thighs, and groaned deeply when he felt how wet she was for him. "Baby, I have to get a condom." He kissed her and started moving away, but she tightened her hands around his neck. He looked down at her, slightly confused. "What's wrong?"

"I'm on the pill." He blinked once at her words, not sure exactly what she was getting at. He was glad she was taking extra precautions. When he didn't respond right away she continued. "You've always used a condom with the girls you've been with?" He swallowed, realizing exactly what she was getting at.

"Yeah, baby." His voice was hoarse, and his dick jumped between them.

"I don't want anything between us. I just want to feel *you*." Mary lifted up and pressed her lips to his. A strangled sound left him when she reached between their bodies, took hold of his cock, and placed it at her pussy.

She lifted her hips, causing the head of his dick to slide inside of her. "*Christ*." He closed his eyes and continued to push into her. Her breath was hard and fast, and when he was fully inside of her he felt her inner muscles clench around him like a vise. "Fucking hell, Mary." Every muscle in his body was taut, and all he wanted to do was fuck her until she knew that she was his.

"Take me, Alex, completely."

That was all he needed to hear her say. Pushing up so his arms were straight right above her head, Alex fucked her like he loved her, and fucking hell he did. Mary was hot and wet, and so fucking tight that sweat immediately popped out along his body.

"God, Mary." He continued moving in and out of her, and before he could tell her how good she felt surrounding him she was the one speaking.

"I love you. I love you so much." They stared at each other, and the emotions that swelled inside of him made him feel high.

"Baby…" His voice cracked, but he never broke eye contact. "I love you, too." God it was fast, so fucking fast, but never had anything felt as good as hearing her say she loved him, or telling her those three words in return. They crashed together, chest to chest, mouth to mouth, and he let everything he felt for her be displayed physically. There was nothing better in the world than being with her, having her scent fill his lungs, and hearing her moan out his name over and over again. He came fast and hard inside of her, following right on the heels of Mary's orgasm. It was the most intense feeling in the world, and he never wanted a barrier between them again. When they were both sated he collapsed on top of her and tried to catch his breath.

"Alex?" Her voice was soft.

"Yeah, baby?"

"I can't breathe." He chuckled and rolled off of her.

"Sorry." Alex pushed a strand of stray hair away from her damp forehead and leaned in to kiss her. "That was…" Shit, he couldn't even describe it.

"Yeah, I know." She smiled up at him, and for the longest time all they did was stare at each other.

"I love you, Mary. And to be honest, it scares me a little bit at how much I do." Yeah, he just said that, and it was one of the most honest things he had ever told another person.

She smiled and lifted her hand to cup his cheek. "I feel the same way, Alex."

He wrapped his arms around her and brought her close.

"Do you want to talk about it?" She had never told him if there was actually something wrong, but he had known in his gut that something had to have happened at dinner tonight.

A pregnant pause filled the air. "There really isn't much to say. I stood up to them. I told Margo what a selfish bitch she was, told my mom I'm not her doll, and told them about Lance and how I will never be with him again." That last part had him stilling.

"Lance, your ex?" Every part of him was tense once again at hearing her say her ex-boyfriend's name. "He was at the dinner?" He leaned away from her so he could look into her face. She looked uncomfortable and nodded.

"Yeah, apparently my mom coincidentally ran into him at the club, but I know Lance planned it, because he called me out of the blue back at campus a few weeks back saying he wanted to see me." That information had his blood rising.

"Wait, he called you?"

"Yeah, before you and I started doing *anything*." She emphasized the last word, and he knew he needed to calm the fuck down. "My mom had this fantasy in her mind that we would get back together, but I cleared that up at dinner. I told them that he was verbally abusive when he drank, that he cheated on me with my friend, all of it."

Well, shit. "What did they say?"

"Nothing, except my normally bland father was pretty pissed at Lance, even told him he was never welcome around them again." *Good.* "But Lance caught up with me in the driveway, and looked ready to kill me."

"He touched you?" Alex didn't hold back the anger in his voice.

She pushed herself up and shook her head. Dammit, all it had taken was the image of that faceless asshole coming near his Mary and he was about to fucking lose it. His blood pressure rose, his muscles contracted, and he forced himself to calm the hell down because he was scaring the woman he loved.

Closing his eyes and taking a deep breath, he said, "I'm sorry, baby, but just knowing that prick was close to you, threatening you, makes me insane." She smiled and snuggled back against his chest, and fuck did it feel good. He didn't even know this guy, but he knew how he had made her feel all those years ago, and that was enough for him to beat the fucker's ass if he ever crossed his path.

"It's okay. Everything is okay now. I'll go to the wedding, but I'm going as myself. I'm going to have you beside me, and I don't care what anyone thinks or says." She tilted her head back and smiled up at him. "If I had known how exhilarating it was to tell them exactly how I felt, and not be bound by my own fear, I would have done it a long time ago."

Alex cupped her cheek. His hand took up one entire side of her face. She was just so small compared to him, but all woman still, and that, coupled with so many other things, made him want to wrap her in his arms and never let her go. But he couldn't smother her, couldn't let his own need to be her protector have her running in the other direction.

"And I'll be right there beside you, letting you lead the way ... sometimes." He winked, and when she laughed it filled the whole room and went straight to his heart.

They took a shower together, one that led to him taking her slowly against the tiles. And then they were back in bed, naked with nothing between them, and the sound of her deep, even breathing lulling *him* to sleep.
****

The wedding had been beautiful, but then again there was no doubt that it would be. Now here Mary was, standing on the stone veranda at the country club where the reception was going on in full swing, thinking. "Stay" by Rihanna played behind her, in an almost haunting tone. She turned and watched as Alex got them drinks from the bar. For some strange and inexplicable reason, her father and Alex had gotten along instantly.

But then again something changed in her father since yesterday. He was still hard and stoic, but there was this softness in his eyes when he looked at her. Had that one incident really broken a part of his tough exterior? She had seen him at the church, and for the first time in longer than she cared to remember, he had embraced her and told her he was proud of her, that he did love her, and that he was sorry for how he made her feel all these years. That had her crying, because it wasn't until that moment that she realized she'd missed hearing him say it. Stephen Trellis was a man of few words and even fewer emotions, and that was how she saw him when she grew up, but when he looked down at her, all she had seen was a father who loved his daughter.

She turned back around and stared at the perfectly manicured grounds with the small intimate lights dotting the trails within the woods surrounding the property. The night was clear, and the glow of the moon washed everything in a silvery hue. Mary let her thoughts drift to her mom and Margo. When she had met them at the salon this morning, she had been surprised to see them standing outside the door, waiting for her. Apprehension had slammed into her, and she knew that whatever was about to be said couldn't be good, not when she hadn't held anything back last night.

But it hadn't been the confrontation she had been expecting. Instead her mother had apologized, and Margo, well Margo had apologized in a way that wouldn't have seemed sincere to anyone that didn't know her. They both told her they hadn't meant to ever make her feel like she didn't belong in the family. It hadn't been this big heartfelt production, but it had been enough for Mary to realize her words last night had gotten through to them. There weren't enough words in the world that would have Mary forget everything that had happened and how everyone had made her feel, but she did want to move forward, and that meant taking the first step.

Now the wedding was over. Margo was now a Barton, and everyone seemed to be on the road to a new start. Mary pushed away from the stone banister and smoothed her hands down the lilac chiffon dress. The bridesmaid gown was elegant and sophisticated, with delicate lace around the bust, and the length falling to her toes. She smiled and made her way back inside, but a deep voice coming from the shadows stopped her.

"Didn't think it would be this easy." The clearly slurred words came from the corner, where the stone outcropping made the shadows thick and visibility nil. Mary tried to see, but it was impossible. Still, she knew that voice and the clearly drunken tone. A second later Lance stepped into the light, the muted glow from the ballroom washing across his disheveled appearance. He was drunk, that much was clear. The scent of a brewery coming from him was enough to have bile rising in her throat.

"You have a lot of balls coming here after I said I wanted nothing to do with you, and my dad said you were no longer welcome."

He smiled, but it was sloppy, just like his appearance. His slacks were wrinkled, and his oxford hung halfway out of his slacks. He looked like shit. His position kept him away from the view of everyone inside, and she would have to get pretty damn close to pass him.

"Just go home and sleep it off, Lance." She didn't even ask how he got in, despite this being a private party. She remembered too many times when he tried to talk her into sneaking in the country club at night to go skinny dipping with his friends. He had been smart enough not to come to Margo's wedding, but certainly had spent that time getting sloshed.

"You know, I thought I'd have to get into some kind of back alley fight with your bodyguard before I could get close to you." He didn't move, and was smart enough to stay away from everyone else's visibility. "I did a lot of thinking today. You owe me a lot, Mary." *Yeah.* Clearly he had done that thinking with a bottle of liquor.

Incredulity washed through her. "Excuse me?" He chuckled, but it was distorted and humorless.

"Yeah, I brought you into my circle, made everyone realize you were even alive. If not for me you'd still be the fucking little Trellis charity case."

"I can't believe I ever found anything appealing about you. You're an asshole, and immature. Go home and sleep it off before you make an even bigger fool of yourself."

She made her way toward the balcony doors, her back straight and her head held high, but before she could enter he had a hold of her hand and roughly pulled her into the shadows. His grip was bruising, and pain lanced up her arm. He spun her around and pressed her against the wall, in the shadowed corner where no light penetrated. Before she could yell for help he slapped his free hand over her mouth. His hot, liquor laced breath wafted across her cheek, and she gagged.

"You made me look like a fucking fool in front of everyone." His forearm was pressed to her throat, cutting off her air and keeping her pressed to the wall. He reached between them and started fumbling with his belt. *Oh, hell no.* She struggled, but in a quick move he had his hand wrapped around her throat. "I think I'll take my anger out on your fucking body." He tightened his hand on her throat, and she clawed at his hold.

He was vile and disgusting, and if she didn't fight harder things would get far worse. The sound of his zipper sliding down seemed loud against the sudden silence that surrounded her. He grunted when she tried to shift out of his hold, but she had to continually lift her hands to her throat, trying to alleviate the suffocating tightness he was delivering.

"I kind of like it when you struggle, Mary." He leaned forward and ran his tongue up her cheek. "Makes me really want to work for it. I should have done this to you when we were dating. It would have made things a lot of a lot better." He grabbed at the bottom of her dress, lifting it up so it pooled around her waist, and then fumbled between them. She tried to twist out of his grasp, kept her legs closed as much as possible, but even drunk he was stronger than she was. His breathing was labored, but she knew it was because this excited him. His erection pressing against her was evidence of that. Mary tried to scream, but the noise came out gurgled. Stars danced in front of her vision from the lack of oxygen, and a moment of fear that he would kill her passed through her mind. Not knowing what else to do she relaxed, hoping to throw him off a bit enough that she could get out of his hold.

"Oh, you want to be a good girl now, Mary?" He loosened his hold slightly, and she breathed in deep, the burning pain enough to have more tears spilling down her cheeks. When he touched her between the legs, it was the vilest sensation. His gaze was glazed over, his mouth parted, and he stared down at what he was doing to her.

This was it, her chance to defend herself while he was distracted. Bringing her knee up she slammed it into his crotch, and loved it when he howled in pain. He let go of her throat so he could cup himself, and she didn't waste a minute to run, but he reached out, grabbed her ankle, and pulled her back.

Mary fell forward and braced her hands on the ground as she went down hard. Pain slammed into her as she landed on her wrist awkwardly, but she couldn't let the agony take her under. The sound of cheering came from inside, and she tried to reach out and catch someone's attention. Lance wouldn't let his guard down again. He pulled her back again, mumbling incoherent words through his teeth and in between grunts of pain. Just when he would have pulled her back into the shadowed corner the balcony doors were opened, and Alex stepped outside.

"Mary? They're getting ready to cut the cake." He held two glasses and looked around for her. Right when Mary opened her mouth to scream for help Alex's gaze landed on hers, and that was when the shit hit the fan. The glasses fell from his grasp and shattered in a million pieces at his feet. The darkness that moved across his face was like nothing she had ever seen, and by the way Lance stopped tugging at her she assumed he saw it as well. Alex charged forward so quickly the next thing she knew was being lifted off the ground and set on one of the chairs off to the side. Her head was fuzzy, her wrist screaming in pain, and her vision cloudy from her tears, but she could still see what was happening right in front of her. Alex had Lance by the throat and dangling in the air. *Oh God.* He looked so powerful and fierce, like some kind of warrior, or dare she say, mythical god.

"You fucked with the wrong girl, asshole." He slammed Lance against the wall and started hitting him in the face over and over again. The sound of bones crunching, of Lance grunting in pain and Alex breathing out in anger, filled her ears. "You're fucking dead." Alex sounded fucking enraged, even possessed.

"Alex." Her throat was raw and felt like she had swallowed fire. "Please, stop."

Alex stopped mid-swing and tightened his hold on Lance's throat. He looked over at her, and the rage in his face intensified. "You want me to stop after what this fucker did to you, Mary?"

Did she? Lance deserved everything he got, but she didn't want to be the cause of it, and she certainly didn't want Alex to be in the thick of it. He held her gaze for a moment, and then let Lance drop unceremoniously to the ground. Lance gasped and sucked in air, but Alex wasn't done. He slammed his fist into his face once more, which caused Lance's head to cock back, blood to pour from his nose, and him to pass out. "You're lucky my girl wanted me to stop."

Everything had seemed to happen at a snail's pace, but Mary knew it had only been a matter of minutes. The commotion drew people out of the ballroom, and they halted when they saw the carnage before them. The light washed over Alex, and when he turned to stare at her she could see blood splattered across his white suit shirt, and that his knuckles were split open. A few men rushed to Lance's side, someone yelled out to call an ambulance, and Mary was only focused on Alex. He was in front of her moments later, taking her face in his hands, and asking her something. She couldn't hear him, just saw his lips moving. The flurry of movement around them couldn't even snap her out of whatever trance she was in.

"Mary." His voice sounded distant, like she was in a tunnel. He called her name again, and the worry on his face had her blinking away the fog that had claimed her. "Mary, baby, please answer me." She looked at his lips, saw a smattering of blood, but didn't feel anything but relief that Alex was there. She burst into tears, unable to control the torrent of emotion that suddenly took over her. "He didn't…" Alex didn't finish that sentence, but then again he didn't have to, because she knew what he was trying to say. Shaking her head because she didn't trust her voice, she fell into his arms and let him comfort her.

"Oh my God." First it was her mother's voice, then Margo's, and then her father was right in front of her, asking her the same question Alex had. Everything seemed to pass in a blur of sounds and movement. Her mother, father, and Margo came up to make sure she was okay, and after she was able to convince them that she was, they gave her enough room to breathe. Once the ambulance took Lance, and the police questioned them, she stared at the perfectly manicured lawn again. She hadn't moved from her spot, but Alex had placed a blanket over her shoulders. The shock had since worn off, and all she felt now was exhaustion and was so very cold. Crawling into bed under a mountain of blankets, locking the world away until she had slept so long and hard all of this vanished, sounded heavenly.

"Baby, are you okay?" Alex sat beside her and wrapped an arm around her shoulder, bringing her close to him. She nodded. She would be. "I am so sorry I wasn't here sooner."

She pushed the blanket off her shoulders and turned so she could look right in his eyes.

"This isn't anyone's fault but Lance's." She heard the police saying something about a broken jaw and nose, but after that she had tuned everything else out. Alex nodded once and helped her stand. He immediately embraced her.

"God, Mary, I love you so much." She gripped his shirt in her hands and rested her head on his chest. Closing her eyes and inhaling his scent deep within her lungs, she felt everything else fade away.

"I love you, too."

They had cleared everyone out while the police and ambulance had shown up, but then Margo had surprised the shit out of her by telling everyone that the reception was over. Now, here she was, with Alex's big arms wrapped around her, his soft, gruff words of affection whispering in her ear, and her family watching the whole thing. She turned slightly in his arms, and couldn't help but smile when he refused to let her go. Her parents, Margo, and Joe stood right inside the ballroom. Her mother was still crying; her father looked as crazy mad as Alex did, and Joe was comforting his frantic wife.

"I think I just want to go to bed." They all stopped talking to each other and looked over at her.

"Honey, are you sure you don't want to go to the hospital?" Her mother sniffed, and her dad gave her a tissue. Her throat was raw and tender, and when she lifted her hand and rubbed her neck her mom cried harder. Mary knew Lance had left a nasty handprint-sized bruise on her flesh.

"I'm fine, really." Charges had been pressed, Lance was at the hospital, but would be facing jail time for assault and attempted rape, and she had Alex and her family beside her to give her support. "I really do just want to go to sleep."

Alex led her out of the reception hall and to his truck. After they left the country club and went back to the hotel room, Mary sat on the edge of the bed. Alex dropped to his knees before her and rested his head in her lap. She speared her fingers through his hair, and was transfixed by the way the dark strands felt like silk. In this position he looked like a defeated man.

"I can't even tell you the rage I felt when I saw you on the ground with him right behind you." She didn't answer, just kept running her fingers through his hair. "I wanted to kill him, Mary." His voice was soft, but deadly. "I would have killed him, too." He lifted his head, and the anguish on his face was tangible. "I also felt hopeless."

"Alex." She didn't know what to say. The situation was fucked up. Lance gone, and she wanted to move forward. She didn't want him running her life any more than he had, and she didn't want him getting between her and Alex. He swallowed loudly.

They didn't need to sit down and talk about their relationship. She wanted him. He wanted her. Nothing else mattered. He stood and wrapped his arms around her and pushed her gently down to the bed. She knew he meant to comfort her with his presence, but she wanted him to help her erase Lance's touch.

"Help me forget, Alex." He lifted his head and stared down at her. He was going to deny her, because she knew any decent man would think they were taking advantage of the situation, but she needed him to touch her, needed his smell all over her, and wanted his voice filling her ears. "I need you, only you. Please, help me get rid of the way he made me feel."

"Baby." He didn't move for a few seconds, but then lowered his face to hers and kissed her softly. The rest, as they say, fell right into place.

Epilogue

Two years later

"Baby, where do you want me to put this one?" Alex stopped in the entryway of their new home, a big box in his arms, and sweat and dirt covering his face and bared arms. He had taken off his shirt an hour ago, and the way his muscles glistened from how hard he was working, and the fact his biceps looked like mountains of muscles, had every part of her warming. Never would she get tired of the sight of him. In fact, she felt the same butterflies in her belly around him as she had when she first saw him all those years ago. She was just as sweaty and dirty as he was, but had decided to take a small break on the sofa and stare out the bay window. The sight wasn't all that gorgeous, just a row of small houses across the street and a few trees, but it was theirs. Saying that never got old.

"You mean the one that says 'Kitchen'? I'm going to take a wild guess and say in the kitchen." She smirked when he glowered. "I mean, I wrote where I wanted the boxes to go when I packed them up." She started laughing at the blank look he gave her.

"You're a smartass, and not funny might I add. I thought these were just old ass boxes with random writing on them. Shit." He finally lost the sour look and grinned. He turned and disappeared, presumably into the kitchen. She rested her head back on the couch and watched as a squirrel ran across the telephone wires across the street. Their small, two bedroom house wasn't anything spectacular, but it was perfect for them. After the whole situation with Lance, Alex had become so protective Mary had to sit down and talk with him, and explain that he couldn't be there at all times, and that yes, she would be all right. It had taken a long time to convince him of that, and even that was only after he made her promise to take self-defense classes, and then proceeded to watch her do said classes. How could she be upset over the fact he just wanted to make sure she was okay? She had graduated last year with her Bachelor's degree, but decided to go back for her Master's. After Alex passed his Human Sexuality course, and thus passed his mid-terms two years ago, he finished out the football seasons and graduated with a degree in sports medicine. Now he worked in a rehab facility as a therapist for sports related injuries. She was so damn proud of him, and so proud of herself for rising above everything and moving forward with her life.

After the incident with Lance, it had opened her parents' eyes. They had changed so much over the past couple of years, and she never thought it would happen, but they actually stated acting like human beings. They realized everything didn't have to revolve around status and money. Margo was still Margo, but her sister called more often to just talk. Mary thought it had to do with her sister's eyes being opened to the fact not everyone was who they seemed, and life really was too short to worry about the petty stuff. She hadn't talked to Lance since the incident, but she had heard he served some jail time, which caused him a lot of problems with the university he attended, and this was a problem his father just couldn't make go away like she was sure he had done for Lance in the past. Aside from that she hadn't heard anything else about him, and didn't care.

Alex came back into the living room and sat beside her on the couch. She wrinkled her nose. "You stink." He nudged her shoulder with his.

"You think you smell like roses, buttercup?" He rested his head on the back of the couch and turned to look at her, grinning. "But I'd still do you, all day long." He let his eyes dip to her breasts, ones that were barely restrained by her tank. He had scowled when she first put it on, but it was damn hot, and hell no was she going to move into their home covered from neck to ankle in clothes, which is probably what he would have preferred. "Did I tell you how hot you look?" She smacked him on the chest but grinned. "You do, even all sweaty. I have a major hard-on right now."

"You're such a pig." He chuckled and leaned in, but she moved out of the way before he could touch her. "No way, you stink."

"Aww, come here, baby. We can stink together." He made a move to grab her, but she jumped off the couch and ran to the other side of it. "We're both sweaty, so let's get dirty together, Mary." She squealed when he hopped over the back of the couch in one move and had her in his arms before she could make a getaway. "Gotcha." He started kissing her throat, and she laughed harder. "Mmm, salty, yet strangely still sweet." She turned so she faced him, wrapped her arms around his neck, and kissed him.

"I love you." She felt him grin against her mouth.

"I know." She broke the kiss and smacked him in the chest again. "I'm just teasing." He kissed her forehead, on the tip of the nose, and finally reached her mouth. "I love you, too, Mary." He lifted her off her feet and started carrying her through the house. "Time to christen the bedroom." He walked into their room and shut the door behind him, and that was exactly what they did, over and over again.

The End

JENIKA SNOW

www.jenikasnow.com

Evernight Publishing

www.evernightpublishing.com

41143582R00120

Printed in Poland
by Amazon Fulfillment
Poland Sp. z o.o., Wrocław